"I haven't had a chance to thank you properly for saving my life. And I'm sorry for being sick on the dock." Her delicate ears reddened, and her gaze dropped.

Uncomfortable, both with being thanked for something he'd done instinctively and with the protective feelings expanding in his chest, he shrugged and half turned away from her. "Don't mention it." He waved away her thanks. "You've seen the most dangerous places on the island. Stay away from the cliff, the fuel stores, and the tower. And it's against the rules for you to enter the lighthouse without one of the keepers. That should keep you safe. And considering the state of this morning's breakfast, I'll stay away from the kitchen. That should keep *me* safe." He grinned, waiting to hear her laugh.

She gasped, dropped her arms to her sides, and stalked off toward the house.

So much for his attempt at humor.

ERICA VETSCH is married to Peter and keeps the company books for the family lumber business. A homeschool mom to Heather and James, Erica loves history, romance, and storytelling. Her ideal vacation is taking her family to out-of-the-way history museums and chatting to curators about local history. She has a bachelor's degree from Calvary Bible College in secondary education: social studies. You can find her on the Web at www.onthewritepath.blogspot.com

Books by Erica Vetsch

HEARTSONG PRESENTS
HP875—The Bartered Bride

The Marriage Masquerade

Erica Vetsch

Heartsong Presents

For my wonderful church family at Cornerstone. Thank you for all your encouragement.

A note from the Author:
I love to hear from my readers! You may correspond with me by writing:

Erica Vetsch
Author Relations
PO Box 721
Uhrichsville, OH 44683

ISBN 978-1-60260-700-2

THE MARRIAGE MASQUERADE

All scripture quotations are taken from the King James Version of the Bible.

All of the characters and events in this book are fictitious. Any resemblance to actual persons, living or dead, or to actual events is purely coincidental.

Our mission is to publish and distribute inspirational products offering exceptional value and biblical encouragement to the masses.

PRINTED IN THE U.S.A.

one

Duluth, Minnesota, April 1906

Noah Kennebrac tilted his head and didn't meet his brother's eyes in the mirror. "I'm through talking about this."

The razor scraped against his cheek, removing thick, brown beard in relentless swatches. The tangy smell of shaving soap mixed with bitterness. His pride lay like the whiskers in the basin, chopped off and scattered. How he'd enjoyed wearing this full beard, the mark of his captaincy. Kennebrae captains always wore a full beard.

"At least tell me where you're going. I need to be able to contact you." Jonathan put his hand on Noah's shoulder.

Noah shrugged off the gesture and rinsed the razor. He cut another patch of whiskers, careful to square off the sideburn. "I can't think why you'd need to contact me. You have everything well in hand."

Habit led him to look out the window toward Lake Superior. The hulk of his first and only command crouched on the shoal where he had grounded it last November. Ice-encased for months, it now rocked with the pounding of the recently freed surf. Jonathan would be out there later today, directing operations. Salvagers would swarm, unloading tons of iron ore, patching the hull as best they could before towing the crippled steamer into the safety of the harbor.

Though Noah mourned the loss of the *Bethany*, he mourned the loss of his crew more. Ten men dead as a direct result of Noah's arrogant foolishness. Only God's mercy had kept the entire complement of sailors from perishing during the storm, including his own brother.

"You should stay here and oversee the salvaging yourself. You're running away, and there's no need." Jonathan rammed his fingers through his hair. "What's happened to you? You've changed so much. This is nonsense."

"Is it? Is it nonsense when no one will look me in the eye? When the widows of my crew members are grieving because I couldn't bring my ship into the harbor? I need a clean break, away from Duluth." Noah's hand trembled, and he lowered the razor. Shame made it difficult to meet his own eyes in the mirror. He set his jaw, gripping the edge of the basin and forcing himself to stare into his reflection, to take the pain he so justly deserved.

Coward. Murderer.

"I know things look dark now, but you wait. Sentiment will change once the salvaging is finished. And I'm sure, once the engineers go over the *Bethany*, you'll be exonerated of any wrongdoing."

Noah snatched up a towel and wiped the excess lather from his face. The sharp smells of soap and cotton pricked his nose, and he fought to relax his gritted teeth.

Again his gaze shot to the window. At least the constant reminder of his failure would be removed from display soon. Not that he would be here to see it. He couldn't take one more day in Duluth—the stares, the whispers, the looks of pity. He had to get away before the guilt ground his soul to powder.

"Is that all you're running from?" Jonathan's stare pierced like a harpoon. "What about the wedding?"

Noah shouldered into his suspenders. "You know my views on that. Just because you fell in love with your arranged bride doesn't mean my marriage would wind up the same. Grandfather will have to break things off since it was his idea in the first place. I don't even know who he had lined up, but it won't matter now. No man is going to want to marry his daughter off to a disgraced ex-captain. I suppose I'm lucky Grandfather let me get out of the hospital and back on my feet before he started nagging about a wedding again. Broken ribs and pneumonia—a blessing in disguise. He'll have to turn his matchmaking schemes on Eli instead. It should be easy. Eli can marry whoever Grandfather chose for me."

Noah headed into his bedroom, rolling down his sleeves and buttoning the cuffs. He swept keys, watch, and coins off the dresser and into his pants pocket.

Jonathan put himself between Noah and the hall door. "Noah, I can't let you go like this. At least tell me where you're headed and when you plan to come back."

Noah noted the square jaw, the glint in his older brother's brown eyes. So much like their grandfather, Abraham Kennebrae. Bossy, dictatorial, sure of himself and his decisions. Noah envied Jonathan his confidence. He hadn't realized what a valuable commodity confidence could be until catastrophe stripped it away, leaving a husk, a shell that threatened to crumble at the first strong wind. "You have to promise you won't tell Grandfather where I am. He'll only want to drag me back and force me into marriage."

"I won't tell him where you've gone, but I will tell him you are all right. You owe him at least that much, to not have to worry after your safety." Jonathan crossed his arms.

Noah lifted his jacket from the bed and shrugged into it. He withdrew a telegram from the breast pocket and handed it to his brother.

Jonathan read the sheet aloud:

APRIL 15, 1906.
NICK KENNEDY

ARRIVE SUTTON ISLAND LIGHT VIA FERRY *JENNY KLAMATH*
APRIL 20 TO ASSUME ASSISTANT KEEPER POSITION *STOP*
STANDARD WAGES UNIFORMS AT YOUR EXPENSE *STOP*
JASPER DILLON – INSPECTOR, US LIGHTHOUSE BOARD

His eyebrows pinched over his nose. "Nick Kennedy?"

Noah stared at the door behind his brother. "You don't think they'd have given me the job if I had applied as Noah Kennebrae, do you? Nick Kennedy is close enough."

"Lying to your employers isn't the best way to start out a new job." Jonathan folded the paper into precise creases and handed it back.

Noah squashed the tickle of guilt Jonathan's accusation sent swirling through his chest. "It isn't a lie. From the moment I walk out that door, I'm Nick Kennedy, assistant keeper of the Sutton Island Light. No past, no manipulating grandfather, and no marriage to a stranger."

"You won't even meet her? At least tell her in person why you won't marry her? It's not like you to cut and run when things get tough."

The barb hit like a shot from a Lyle gun.

"Running is never the answer." Jonathan stepped aside, lines of sorrow etching his face.

Noah swallowed hard and picked up his seabag. "All I know is I can't stay here. I have to get out."

"When will you come back?"

"I don't know." Maybe never. When he could look his crew members in the eyes and not feel he'd let them down. When he could sleep through the night without nightmares of being frozen to death in his own pilothouse. When he found some way of getting through a day without wishing he had perished in the storm folks were now calling the *Bethany Blow*.

❧

Anastasia Michaels pounded up the curved staircase in an unladylike manner. She rushed down the hall to her bedroom and skidded inside. The door slammed with a *thud*, and she sagged against it, her hand still clutching the knob.

Hazel looked up from the rocker beside the fireplace. Her needle hovered over yards of white nightgown material.

"What is it this time, child?" Hazel had a dried-apple

face, her eyes gleaming like two pips amid the wrinkles. She regarded Anastasia with a calm, unruffled expression. Nothing Anastasia did seemed to rile the woman who had looked after her for all of her nineteen years.

Anastasia panted, one hand on her chest, breathless more from her news than from running through the halls of Michaelton House. "Father's home from Hibbing. He went right into the study with an old man in a wheelchair. He didn't even greet me after being away for months. And do you know what they were talking about?"

Hazel eyed her shrewdly. "And how is it you overheard them if they went into the study?"

Anastasia's ears tingled with heat, and she twisted her hands at her waist. "Well, I walked by the door, and my shoe was unfastened. I had to bend over, and it just happened to bring my ear down to the keyhole. . . ."

Hazel's eyebrows lifted.

"Oh Hazel, now isn't the time to chide me for eavesdropping. It's the only way to find out anything around here. Father and that man are hatching the most awful plan." She flung her arms wide.

Hazel ran her gnarled hand across the fabric in her lap and resumed her mending. "It can't be as bad as all that. I've told you eavesdropping only gives you part of the story. Your father is an upstanding businessman. He wouldn't be doing anything underhanded."

"But he is!" Anastasia plopped onto the footstool beside the rocker and anchored her elbows onto her knees, her hands providing a perch for her chin. "They're downstairs right now arranging my marriage. To a stranger—the grandson of the man in the wheelchair. They're discussing me as if I was a company asset. Father is talking about mergers and gross tonnage and quarterly profits. And the other man is just as bad. He's gloating over railcars, loading docks, and net worth. It's disgusting."

The lines around Hazel's lips deepened, her eyes dimming. "So the time has come."

Anastasia sat up and gripped the edges of the footstool. "You don't seem surprised." Her heart fluttered like a captured bird. "Please tell me you didn't know about this." She frowned at Hazel.

Hazel poked the needle in and out furiously.

"Why didn't you tell me?"

"Your father forbade me to tell you, Annie." No one but Hazel ever called her Annie. "He told me months ago so I could look for another place if I chose. Once you're married there will be no need for me. Your husband will no doubt have his own staff. If I don't want to find a new position, your father will retire me to a cottage he owns in Hibbing to live out my days."

"How is it he wanted you to be prepared and spared no thought to warning me?" Anastasia bounded up to pace the rug. "Who has he chosen? How could he know what kind of man would be a good match for me? He's so wrapped up in his business he barely knows what I look like. He spends all his time at his mines, then the first time he's home in months, he's making plans to rid himself of me."

Hazel set aside the mending and rose, her shoulders stooped with age but her step light. "I don't see what you can do about it, child. Your father has worked out the legal details. They'll be setting a wedding date now, I imagine. That was the last thing to do once your father got back to Duluth."

"I'll just show you what I can do about it. I'll march right down there and tell both those old schemers what they can do with their old wedding plans." She headed to the door, hands fisted at her sides.

Hazel grabbed Anastasia's elbow. "Annie, you'll just embarrass yourself and anger your father. Their plans won't be set aside by your tantrums."

"But what else can I do?" Hot tears pricked her eyes. How could he do this to her? Why wouldn't he even consult her before signing her away like one of his business contracts? He never would have treated her brother, Neville, like this. Not his son and heir. "Hazel, won't you help me?" She gripped her hands together, trying to calm her jangling nerves and think.

Hazel's eyes swept Anastasia, her wrinkled face softening into gentle lines. "Don't you even want to meet the young man? He might be nice, you know."

Anastasia waved her hands, pushing the idea away. "No, I don't want to meet him. What kind of man lets someone else decide his future? Not the kind I want to marry, that's for sure. I spent my entire childhood trying to earn Father's respect and love, and he ignored me. If I let him choose my husband, he'll pick someone just as cold and unfeeling. I can't live like that. I can't live without love."

"How do you plan to get out of this then?"

"I'll get a job. Maybe as a seamstress or a governess or something." She threaded her fingers through the heavy, blond curls lying on her shoulder. She knew precious little about sewing or caring for children, but she'd rather do that than be shackled to a stranger for the rest of her life. And Anastasia could count on Hazel for help, as she always had. She just had to wait for it.

Hazel tapped her pursed lips, eyeing Anastasia. "You're so much like your mother. Twenty-five years ago I stood in her bedroom having very nearly this same conversation. She was forced into marriage with Philip Michaels, a perfect stranger. I couldn't do anything to help her. But I will try to help you now."

two

Damp, chilly air swirled around Anastasia off Lake Superior. A faint red pinstripe of dawn marked the horizon. She took one last look around her opulent bedroom, hiked her skirts, and lifted her leg over the sill of her third-story window.

Her boot toe poked the air. She eased farther out the window, her fingers already aching from their death grip on the frame. Hazel's brilliant plan, hatched a week ago, didn't seem so brilliant now. But if Anastasia could just get out of the house without any of the servants seeing her, she would have crossed the most precarious of many bridges.

Stop wool-gathering and get going, girl. Time's running out.

Unable to reach the ledge, she bit her lip and eased both legs outside, rolling over until her stomach pressed against the sill. If people passed on the street below, they'd be treated to a scandalous view of her backside hanging from the window.

Scrape.

One toe ticked the rock ledge. Anastasia squirmed backward a few precious inches. Ah, at last. She slid her torso down, smacking her hat against the sash, shoving the bonnet over her eyes.

"Botheration." Curls bounced off her forehead and cheek. She pushed the hair out of the way, trying to tuck it behind her ear and right her hat at the same time, all while clinging one handed to the outside of Michaelton House. Madam DeVries of the Duluth Ladies' Academy would have a fainting spell if she could see Anastasia now.

She steadied her breathing. First hurdle almost complete. Every muscle tense, she inched around until she faced away from the window. Strings of yellow light hung like vapors to the east.

The romance of the moment wasn't lost on her. She could be a heroine from one of those dime novels the maids liked to giggle over. Brave, intrepid, willing to risk everything for love. . .or in her case, freedom. She closed her eyes and breathed deeply.

Hooves clopping on the street jarred her back to reality. She froze until the wagon passed, grateful the driver didn't look up.

Hurry, girl.

Step, *scrape*, step, *scrape*. Her derrière scratched against the rough stone blocks of her home. If she could cross to the conservatory roof, she could ease down the gentle copper slope to the ground.

Anastasia almost laughed when she drew near the greenish metal, relief making her giddy. She took stock, squinting in the poor light to make out the best place to put her feet. Hazel's sturdy boots weighed at her feet and ankles, so unlike the dainty footgear she normally wore.

"Oh Lord, help me." She probed with a toe until she found a purchase on the slippery rooftop. So far so good. She reached for the ridgepole to steady herself, wrapping her chilly fingers on the folded metal seam.

Whump!

Her feet slid out from beneath her, and she landed on her hip, sliding, scrabbling, rushing toward the rain gutter.

A scream crowded into her throat, but she clamped her lips closed. Her eyes slammed shut as her body launched over the edge of the roof into the air. She hit the ground hard, the impact shoving the breath from her lungs and rattling her teeth. She forced her eyes open. Her backside throbbed and her wrist stung, but everything else seemed intact. Had anyone heard her?

Lamplight shone from the basement windows. The staff

was up and stirring, lighting fires, preparing breakfast, but no cries of alarm or inquiry and no movement in the yard.

Dampness seeped through her heavy wool coat from the slush lying under the eaves. Her hands tingled with cold. She choked back a groan as she pushed herself up from the crocus and daffodil spears. At least she hadn't landed amongst the lilacs. Those would have been much less forgiving. A few swipes at her skirt and another adjustment to her hair and hat fortified her dignity and bolstered her courage.

Hazel's battered carpetbag lay behind the forsythia bushes along the foundation, just where Hazel had stashed it the night before. Anastasia grunted at the weight, bumping the bag against her legs and staggering across the grass toward the driveway. Hazel had sent Anastasia's trunk ahead to the docks the night before, but the valise bulged with all the things Anastasia didn't think she could do without. Next time she would pack lighter.

A chuckle escaped her lips. What next time? If this scheme failed, she'd be locked up tighter than the crown jewels until her wedding.

Her wedding. Ha! Her sentencing, more like. Father hadn't broached the subject with her, not in the entire week he'd been home. In fact, he'd barely spoken to her, closing himself up in his study when he was home and spending most evenings at his club. But whoever her intended might be, if her father approved of him, he must be deadly dull and proper. Probably not an ounce of adventure or imagination in him.

She crept along the lilacs bordering the curved drive, keeping as close to the branches as possible. She would miss the flowering of the hedge this spring.

A bit of tension eased when she reached the road. Moist pavement gritted under her boots. Duluth and Lake Superior spread out before her. Michaelton House stood atop Skyline

Parkway, looking down into the lake basin—not as fashionable a location as the mansions right on the lake, but her father preferred the hilltop view.

Built just six years before, Michaelton House dominated the block with its turrets and garrets, dormers and slate roof. It looked the castle of Anastasia's dreams. Her throat squeezed at the thought of leaving Hazel and all that was familiar. The urge to go back clambered up her ribcage.

Firming up her resolve, she hurried down the block to catch the first streetcar of the morning. A grocer's cart rumbled by, making the morning deliveries, followed by the milkman's blue and white truck. Bottles clinked and rattled. The driver tipped his cap to her. She nodded, ducked her chin, and hurried on.

Anastasia had never been out this early before. Several people waited on the corner. Men in rough coats, smelling of cigar smoke and sausage. Women in plain dresses, noses pink in the chilly air, waiting for the tram to take them to their cleaning or manufacturing jobs.

Anastasia tucked herself into the back of the group so she didn't have to make eye contact with anyone. She clutched the valise handle with both hands, staring at the sidewalk. Her pulse throbbed in her throat. Concentrating on just the next step, the next obstacle, she pushed away the thought of the biggest challenge yet ahead. For now, just boarding the streetcar, making three switches, and getting to the harbor seemed enough. She half expected someone from home to grab her and haul her back at any second.

After an age of waiting, the tram pulled up to the corner. She barely glanced at the driver or the horses. Keeping her head down, she swung herself aboard. Public transportation, another first today. Dockworkers and domestic help crowded the plain wooden seats, the smell of damp wool and sack lunches clinging to them. Anastasia had an overwhelming sense of standing out like a beacon.

She dug into her pocket for her coin, alarm shooting through her when she didn't find it right away. At last her fingers closed around it in the corner of her pocket. She dropped it into the box and edged down the center aisle, thankful for Hazel's coaching.

The bell clanged, startling her as she thumped down onto a seat. She settled her valise in her lap and placed her feet close together, tucking them as far back under the seat as she could.

A burly man with a mustache that made him look like he'd been eating a bristle broom lurched into the seat across from her. He smelled of sausage and syrup.

The tram started down the steep slope to the lake, stopping every couple of blocks to disgorge and take on more passengers. After three stops, she dared look out the window. The sun painted the business district in soft pinks and golds, burning away the low-lying fog. Businessmen in dark topcoats entered stone buildings through brass and glass doors, the commerce of Duluth waking to life.

Anastasia transferred to a cross-town streetcar, praying she had done the right thing. She should've written down Hazel's directions instead of trying to commit them to memory.

By the time she transferred to the harbor tram, she felt like a seasoned public transportation traveler. She got off at the ferry dock. A fresh breeze whipped her cheeks and tugged at her hair. Water slapped against the pilings, restless, as if seeking a way to climb the dock. She looked over the side of the quay at the chopping waves, her head swirling and her stomach churning.

Her heart thudded at what she was about to do. Could she force herself to get on a boat? Fear tightened her throat until she thought she would suffocate. Finally, air rushed into her lungs. She gasped, placing her hand on her chest, trying to quell the panic. Her arms prickled with heat, while her hands went cold. Instantly, she was a shivering six-year-old, dripping, gasping, clinging to the upturned bottom of a rocking rowboat.

≈

"Nick, pass me the wrench, will you?" A gnarled hand jutted from beneath the diesel engine.

Nick looked up from the bucket of gasoline. Greasy parts sloshed in the pungent liquid. He dug in the tool chest, implements clanking. "Think we'll get her put back together before dark? I don't fancy pumping those foghorns up by hand all night if a bank rolls in." He slapped the handle of the wrench into the grimy palm.

Fingers closed around the crescent wrench and disappeared under the engine once more. Between grunts and metallic bangs, the voice of his boss, Ezra Batson, drifted out. "We'll get her put right. Just needed a new seal. You finished washing the grease off those parts?"

"Almost." Nick gave them a final swish then tossed them onto a flannel rag. The gasoline evaporated quickly in the sunshine slicing through the door. He pulled another cloth from his back pocket and wiped his hands. "How often does the fog-engine break down? I've been here a week and this is the third time we've worked on her." He didn't really mind. The release his spirit felt at leaving Duluth made him take small annoyances like broken machinery in stride. The more he got used to being Nick Kennedy, the less he felt the drag of Noah Kennebrae's recent problems. He found himself smiling more, even able to tease a bit. How odd to feel like a new man and yet feel like his old self all at the same time.

Ezra scooted across the concrete floor on his back, emerging into the light. Grease smeared his cheek and dirt flecked his gray hair. "It's just working out the kinks, since the equipment sits idle all winter." He rubbed his nose with the back of his hand. "Takes a lot of maintenance to stay on top of things.

I can't tell you how glad I am the Lighthouse Board sent you and the boy along this year. Last year I had to make do with one helper who quit after a month. Said it was too remote out here. He was lonely for the lights of Duluth."

Nick sorted through the parts, fitting some together, lining up nuts and bolts for reassembling the engine cover. "I guess what some see as a burden, others see as a blessing."

Ezra tossed the wrench into the toolbox and rolled to his knees to stand. "You don't seem to mind it, that's sure. I'd think a handsome young feller like you would have a lady at home missing him."

Only some well-heeled heiress Grandfather wants to shove at me. He shrugged, shaking his head. "No lady at home. I think I'm destined to be a bachelor forever. I like peace and quiet."

His boss chuckled. "That's what they all say until the right girl comes along and knocks all their previous notions into the lake. Mark my words, son, if you meet the right girl, you'll never be the same."

Nick inserted a bolt and spun a nut on the shaft. "Maybe you got the last, best girl." He smothered a grin, anticipating Ezra's answer.

"I got the best one, that's a fact." The old man's face softened, his eyes going warm as they did whenever he talked about his wife. "Imogen's a treasure. Like the Good Book says, 'Her price is far above rubies,' and I wouldn't trade her, not even for an ore boat of gems." He walked to the door and stared out at the lake, his eyes squinting in the bright light glinting off the restless waves. "This year will be easier on my Imogen. The Board is sending a woman out to help with the housekeeping and cooking. Should arrive on the *Jenny Klamath* this afternoon." He palmed his pocket watch. "In an hour or so, if they're running on time. I want you and Clyde to meet the ferry. You can pick up the mail and tote this woman's baggage up to the house."

A woman? *Hmm.* That would be good for Mrs. Batson.

Though neither Ezra nor his wife ever spoke of it in Nick's hearing, he had a feeling Mrs. Batson was ailing somehow. Her skin had a transparent, papery look to it, and Ezra had mentioned her trouble with headaches. Nick wondered at his boss for bringing her to such an inaccessible spot. She looked like she needed to be under a physician's care, not marooned on a rock in the middle of Lake Superior, miles from shore and leagues from a hospital.

"Hope this lady's better than the last one they tried." Ezra handed Nick another bolt from the cloth on the floor. "Don't know where she hid the liquor, but she managed to get some here to the island. That gal was drunk as a skunk from noon till dark every day. And she sang when she was drunk, songs no woman should know. And when her liquor ran out, she got mean. Imogen tried to help her, but she wasn't having any. We put up with her for two weeks, till the *Jenny Klamath* made her return trip down-lake; then I packed her up and sent her back to Duluth. I can't abide a drunk, and a drunk woman's even worse."

Nick tried to imagine the upright and steadfast Ezra faced with a rollicking drunk in his kitchen. A smile tugged at his lips. "Sounds like you were better off without her. Surely the Lighthouse Board will have found someone more suitable this time."

Ezra grunted. "I think they jump at anyone willing to come here. Sometimes I don't think they even interview these ladies. I've heard stories that would curl your hair. Women running from the law, women with compromised morals looking to find a lonely lighthouse keeper to latch onto. If we didn't need the help, I never would've applied for a housekeeper in the first place. But there's no way Imogen could keep things up to the mark. Not with inspections being like they are."

"The inspector's pretty thorough?" Nick tightened the last bolt and began cleaning up the tools.

"Hear my words: Jasper Dillon is the most thorough, most disagreeable inspector the Lighthouse Board has ever employed. Most folks just talk about a white-gloved inspection. Dillon actually does them. Everything on this rock is owned by the Board, but Dillon acts like it belongs to him personally. Every windowsill, every pane of glass, every blade of grass on Sutton Island will be inspected for cleanliness and adherence to the code set forth by the Board. Sometimes I think Dillon must sleep with that book under his pillow. He's got every line memorized, and he enforces every rule to the maximum."

Nick's eyebrows rose. "That bad, huh? How often does he come to inspect?"

"That's the trouble. There's no schedule. He just pops up like a summer squall, blows in, wreaks havoc and threatens to fire us all, then blows out. It might be a month from now or it might be this afternoon. But he'll come. And if he finds anything out of order, he'll be back with a vengeance the next time."

"He sounds charming. I can't wait to meet him." Nick grinned.

"Don't take him lightly." Ezra's frown brought Nick up short. "When you see him coming, you'd best scramble into your uniform coat and look smart. He's not a man to trifle with."

Nick pursed his lips, bringing his hand up to stroke his beard. He stopped when his fingers touched his bare cheek, a wry smile twisting his lips. When was he going to stop doing that? "We'd best test this engine out. I can only imagine what would happen if Inspector Dillon showed up and it wasn't working."

The engine turned over and rumbled to life, the sound filling the small fog-house, making conversation impossible. Nick watched the needle on the pressure gauge rise, pressure building in the cylinder. When it reached the right level, the twin foghorns on the roof bellowed out a long *beeee-yoooooouuuu*. Nick grinned at Ezra who killed the engine.

In the silence, a steam-whistle blast piped across the water, a cheerful and impertinent echo of the mighty foghorn. Ezra stuck his head out the doorway, shading his eyes to see down-lake. "It's the ferry. You best go meet her. I'll finish up here and see you at the house."

Nick rolled down his sleeves and plucked his hat from a peg on the wall. He'd best look presentable to meet this new housekeeper. He checked his appearance, whisking some dirt from his pant leg. At least his boots gleamed. He'd spent most of last night rubbing them with mink oil to waterproof them, then applying polish and elbow grease to buff them to a glossy shine. An inspector would find nothing to quibble about there.

three

Annie clutched her valise to her quivering stomach and wished for the thousandth time she had never set foot on the *Jenny Klamath*. Why did this have to be the first job to present itself? Why hadn't something come along where she could keep her feet on dry land?

Mist coated her clothing and hair. She closed her eyes, willing herself not to be sick. The gentle rise and fall of the ferry played havoc with her senses, sending waves of pea green clamminess sloshing through her. She tried to make herself one with the bench.

The ship's whistle pierced the air, laughing at her frailty. She jerked, her eyes popping open. Cold sweat bathed her skin, her neck and back aching with tension. If only this nightmare would end. She dared a look out of the corner of her eye, not moving her head. Purplish grey cliffs rose ahead of the ferry, white surf pounding their jagged, rock-strewn edges. Dark trees poked the sky high overhead, and looming above that, sunlight shattering off its prisms, the red and white tower of the Sutton Island Light.

Annie swallowed hard, forcing down her rising gorge. *Almost there. Almost there. Almost there.* The chant, growing faster to match her heart rate, swirled in her ears.

Around her, crew members prepared to pull into the dock, shouting to one another, swarming over the lashed-down cargo as if they hadn't a care in the world. Lines whizzed through the air, and at last, the ferry bumped softly into the dock.

Thank You, Lord. Thank You, Lord.

"Miss Fairfax?" A crewmember stopped in front of her.

"Sutton Island, miss."

She nodded, trying to smile, though her cheeks refused to budge. Her breath caught against the lump in her throat. Time to go. She inched forward on the hard bench. Weakness spiraled down her legs.

With a death grip on the rail, she baby-stepped along the deck. Her head swam with nausea. She reached the gap in the rail where the gangway was supposed to be. Open space down to restless blue green water yawned before her. No gangway? How was she supposed to reach the dock?

"Toss your bag down, ma'am." The deckhand stood at her elbow. When she didn't move, he took the valise from her grasp and heaved it across the chasm. It landed on the dock safe and sound.

A tall young man stood beside her bag, looking up at her. "Afternoon, Jenkins. This the new housekeeper for the light?" He scrutinized her, the breeze ruffling his dark hair. She couldn't read his expression, but his close observation did nothing to quell her fears or her queasy stomach.

"This is her. Give her a hand down, will you? I need to make sure the boys offload all the mail. Last time they forgot two packages."

"Sure." The man held up his hand to Annie. "C'mon, miss. I'll help you."

They expected her to leap across open water? Were they mad? She'd fall in and be sucked under the dock. "I can't." She shook her head, her hands icy. Tremors of weakness flowed down the backs of her legs.

He rolled his eyes. "I don't have all day. I have work to do."

She squeezed the rail harder, tears of fear and frustration pricking her eyes. "I can't. It's too far." Her voice rasped in her dry mouth.

The man blew out a long breath and swung aboard the ferry. She both marveled at and resented his casual grace all in the same instant. Without warning, he scooped her up into his arms.

She squealed, grasping him about the neck. "Sir, what are you—"

Ignoring her, he leaped. His boots thumped on the boards, and wondrously, the pitching and rocking stopped. Annie looked over his shoulder at the ferry then into his eyes—blue, the same color as the sky. He set her down and backed up a pace, looking over her head up the dock.

Relief at being off the boat surged through her, relaxing her icy control. "Thank you, sir. I'm so—" To her complete and utter mortification, she lost the fight with her nausea and retched on the man's immaculate black boots.

His jaw slacked, his eyes going wide. He looked at his boots then at her.

She clapped her hand over her mouth. "I—I–I'm so sorry."

He didn't move, blinking in shock.

She backed away. Embarrassment flooded her cheeks with heat. Humiliated, she whirled and ran up the dock.

Someone's laughter chased at her, mocking.

Halfway to shore, something rocketed into her side, flinging her through the air. She screamed, arms flailing, grasping for something, anything to hold on to, but finding nothing. Her backside smacked the water, and the icy lake closed over her head.

ও

A scream ripped through the air.

Nick looked up from his ruined boots to see the lady responsible sailing over the side of the dock. Clyde Moore let the mailbag drop to the ground. It took Nick a moment to realize Clyde must've sideswiped the new housekeeper with the bag and pitched her into the water.

Nick ran, dodging ferrymen. When he reached the spot where she'd gone in, he peered into the water. Nothing. He flung off his hat then heaved off his boots. "Get a rope ready, you fools! Clyde, launch the boat!"

Nick leaped feet first into the frigid waves, tucking his knees up when he hit the water, trying to jump shallow so as not to hit any submerged rocks. The icy water sucked his breath away, instantly numbing his fingers and toes. He took a deep breath then went under, hands wide and grasping. He scraped his knuckles on a boulder. The surf slammed him into the base of the cliff.

For eternal seconds he peered through the murky green water, arms sweeping, legs forcing him to go deeper along the cliff. Waves pummeled him. His lungs screamed for air, even while his feet went numb. He could feel his strength being sapped by the cold.

At the moment when he knew he must surface, something soft tangled around his fingers. He grabbed a fistful of cloth. He turned toward the surface, pushing off a rock to gain momentum, dragging her after him. She gave him no help, limp as a rug. It was probably too late. Of all the stupid accidents, falling off a dock.

His head broke the surface, and he sucked in a great lungful of air. The girl's face lolled out of the water on his shoulder, her mouth open, eyes closed. He wrapped his arms around her middle and squeezed. Water gushed from her mouth, her eyes popped open, and she moaned. Relief surged through him at her coughing and wheezing. She wasn't dead, at least not yet.

He spun in the water to locate the dock. The current had taken them more than twenty yards away and they were getting farther all the time. Nick swiped at her long, clinging hair that tangled across his face, obscuring his vision.

Men swarmed the dock, scrambling to get the lighthouse rowboat launched.

The girl seemed to suddenly become aware of her circumstances. She stiffened, screamed loud enough to drown a foghorn, and tried to climb on top of him. His head went under, water filling his nose and eyes and ears. She clawed at him, flailing and swinging. Her elbow connected with his cheekbone, sending stars exploding through his vision. Stupid girl would drown them both.

When he resurfaced he clamped his arms around her, pinning her flailing limbs to her sides. "Stop it, you little fool!"

She seemed not to hear him, screaming and going under, writhing as he tried to kick hard enough to keep them above the waves. His shoulder hit a submerged rock, and his grip on her loosened. He reached out for the rock with one hand, the other grasping her wrist, tugging her toward him. White ringed her eyes, her hair straggling over her face and shoulders. He could barely feel her wrist in his grasp. The rock allowed him a moment's breather, even as a wave splashed over them.

When she screamed again, he did something he had never contemplated before. He let go of the rock for an instant and slapped her with his open hand across her cheek.

Stunned, her scream died. He used the moment to pull her toward him again, clinging to the rock. She subsided. Had he knocked her senseless?

Oars smacked the water, and before she could regroup for another bout at drowning him, Clyde's face appeared over the edge of the rowboat.

"Take her." Nick knew his lips must be blue, they were so stiff. Strong arms lifted the woman over the side of the boat. They reached back down for him, and to his shame, he was too cold to assist himself. They lifted him like a child and settled him in the rocking craft. The wind on his wet skin and clothes bit colder than the lake. His teeth chattered, his muscles cramping.

"Hang on, Nick."

He huddled on the bottom of the boat, shivers wracking him. The woman lay only inches from him, eyes closed, skin white as new snow. Hanks of gold hair clung to her pale features, and her long lashes, gathered in points by the water, lay against her cheeks. Her chest rose and fell in short gasps. At least she was still alive. Which was more than he could say for the way he felt.

"Almost there, Nick." Clyde swung the oars to turn the boat alongside the pilings.

Strength trickled back, sending pins and needles into his hands and feet. Nick stumbled onto the dock. Someone threw a jacket around his shoulders. He brushed him aside, teeth chattering. "Take care of the girl."

Clyde lifted her, still limp, onto the boards. Jenkins appeared with a blanket to cover her.

"Got to get her. . .up the hill." Nick shoved his dripping hair out of his eyes, his hand trembling. Shivers wracked him until he thought he'd never get his boots back on. His soiled boots seemed a small matter now. He struggled into them, the leather sticking to his wet socks and legs.

The *Jenny Klamath* gave a toot of the whistle. The captain eased her away from the dock, evidently intent on keeping his schedule, a near drowning or not. Jenkins swung aboard at the last moment, waving back at Nick with an apologetic smile.

Clyde and Nick loaded the woman onto the handcart used to haul supplies up the track to the lighthouse at the top of the cliff. Nick sneezed and coughed, his lungs protesting their dunking. Silt stung his eyes, blurring his vision. Frigid water dripped from his clothes. They lifted the cart handle and began the trek through the trees, the iron tracks of the cart path glinting where the sunlight dappled through the pines.

four

Annie pressed her hand against her chest, coughing. Her hair hung in dripping rats' tails. Every movement brought an unpleasant gush of water from her clothing and shoes. But nothing could compare to the guilt and embarrassment sloshing through her. As if it wasn't bad enough to throw up on someone, she had to nearly drown him.

The cart rumbled and bumped over the ground, winding up a steep grade through trees and into the open. The wind rippled over her, chill fingers stroking her skin. She lay shivering, her body wracking with cold.

The two men stopped the cart before a two-story brick house. The younger one, red hair blazing, grinned at her. The older one, her rescuer, reached into the cart and scooped her up like a child. What little breath she had fled. She should say something, protest that she could make her own way up the steps, but her teeth chattered so hard she couldn't form the words. His arms held her secure, and she found her eyes closing, her head tipping to lie against his shoulder.

His boots clomped on the steps. Then a screen door squeaked and banged shut. She really should pay attention, but all she could concentrate on was the cold.

"Oh, dear, what happened?"

Annie's eyes flew open. A tiny, white-haired woman with dark eyes stood beside the stove.

"This is the new housekeeper. She fell in the lake."

Indignation rose in Annie's chest. She had *not* fallen in. She was pushed.

Before she could say anything, her rescuer continued. "I'll leave her to your care, Imogen. And you might want to give

28

her something for a bilious stomach. She doesn't seem to have taken too well to boat travel." Without another word, he dumped—well, eased—her into a straight-backed kitchen chair and strode out the door, like a man glad to be done with an unpleasant task.

The screen door squeaked again, and the redheaded fellow tossed Annie's valise in where it landed with a *thump*. "There's a trunk at the dock with your name on it. I'll fetch it up as quick as I can." A flash of white teeth and a multitude of freckles and he was gone.

The elderly woman tut-tutted, stoking the fire and pulling the teakettle forward. "Oh, you poor thing. You must get into dry things immediately. Let's get you up to your room. I'm Imogen Batson. What a poor welcome you've had."

Annie followed her employer up the stairs. Imogen took each step slowly. Annie couldn't help but wonder what such a delicate and fragile woman was doing at a lighthouse station.

"Now, you get into dry clothes and come down for a hot cup of tea." Imogen showed her into the bedroom. "I'm sorry. I don't know your name."

"Ana—Annie. Annie Fairfax, Mrs. Batson."

"Pleased to meet you, Annie. Call me Imogen. We don't stand on much ceremony around here." Imogen closed the door behind her.

Water dripped in a circle from Annie's skirts. Weariness rolled over her, making her fingers clumsy. She peeled the drenched clothes off and let them fall in a sodden heap. Two coarse towels hung on the back of the washstand. She plucked them off, rubbing her skin hard to restore circulation. Then she rummaged through her valise. When she couldn't find what she sought, she dumped the contents onto the bed in a jumble.

Dressed again, though sans her soggy shoes, she draped a towel over her shoulders to keep her wet hair off her blouse and ventured downstairs.

Imogen waited in the parlor. "You sit here by the fire, and I'll get you some hot tea."

As she warmed by the fire with the cup of tea Imogen prepared for her, shame spread over Annie. The man who saved her life—that poor man she'd almost killed—had dumped her on Imogen like a puppy that had been naughty on the rug.

"How are you feeling, dear? Such a dreadful thing to happen, falling in the lake like that. It's a wonder you survived. God was surely looking out for you, having Nick close by. A blessing, it was." Imogen tucked a hot water bottle into the chair beside Annie and pulled an afghan up around her shoulders. "The water's terribly deep there at the base of the cliff. And it's not long since ice-out."

Annie breathed in the aroma rising from her teacup. So his name was Nick. It suited him. "I'm not sure he would share your opinion." Her teeth only rattled a little against the porcelain. After all the trauma of the day, Annie had no more energy than a dust rag. Her escape from Michaelton House early that morning seemed to have happened in another lifetime.

"I have a feeling we're going to do well together, you and I." Imogen patted Annie's shoulder. "Are you warming?"

"Yes, thank you." Annie smiled. Imogen reminded her a bit of Hazel: kind, uncomplicated, easy to be around, by turns starchy and sweet. Perhaps this job wouldn't be so hard after all. Her fears of getting a mean taskmistress of an employer seemed unfounded.

Imogen took the chair across from Annie and picked up her tatting. The shuttle poked in and out of the white lace slowly in the older woman's hands.

How many times had Hazel tried to teach Annie to tat? Annie had no patience for handwork—snarling thread and pricking her finger more than she stitched. She'd rather read a book, taken away to exotic, exciting places in her imagination, than in the words of the old nursery rhyme to "sit on a cushion and sew a fine seam." Hazel had relented and done the sewing for Annie, allowing Annie to read aloud while Hazel worked.

Homesickness weighed her shoulders. When would she see Hazel again? When would she sit beside a fire and read aloud to someone eager to hear the adventure of a good book? She shook her head to clear her thoughts. "Do you think Nick will be all right?"

Imogen nodded. "He's a tough one, that Nick Kennedy. And private. Keeps to himself most of the time. But a good worker. My Ezra says he's never seen a man so careful to follow all the rules. Never shirks a duty. I doubt a dunking will set him back."

Annie breathed a prayer of relief. Though the accident wasn't her fault—after all, she'd been knocked into the water by a flying mailbag—she would hate to think she'd caused her rescuer any permanent damage. She couldn't bear something like that to happen to her again. Echoes of the panic she'd felt when she hit the water fluttered through her. All her worst fears and memories collided, and she had to force herself to breathe slowly. She set her cup aside, afraid she might drop it.

"Imogen, please tell me about my duties here." Her gaze traveled over the simple parlor, noting the rag rugs, the white lace curtains, the brown sofa and chairs, everything clean and shining. So normal and ordinary, it calmed Annie once more.

"Oh, you don't want to hear about that now. Time enough in the morning to start work."

"No, really, I'd rather know now. Otherwise, I won't sleep well wondering." Annie didn't want to admit she had no idea what tasks a housekeeper might do in a place like this. The housekeeper at home walked around like a prison warden, keys jangling from the chatelaine on her belt, a permanent persimmon pucker on her lips as if disapproving of even the air she breathed. The maids scurried at the sight of her, and only the butler remained undaunted by her ramrod posture and formidable face. Annie avoided her as much as possible. Hazel and the housekeeper were at permanent daggers drawn where Annie's room and possessions were concerned.

"There's the cooking, the cleaning, and the laundry—those are the main things. Then we do a bit of gardening, and if need be, we help with the light. The light comes first here, always. From dusk to dawn the beacon must shine." A gentle smile creased her face. "You'll come to love Old Sutton. I've lived around lighthouses so long I find it difficult to rest comfortably unless I fall asleep to the steady flash of a beacon."

Annie didn't care about the light at that moment. Her thoughts centered on one thing—cooking. There was no cook here? Cleaning she could probably do—dusting, even mopping—but cooking? Annie had never so much as boiled water for tea before. How was she supposed to cook meals?

Don't panic, girl. You can do this.

Perhaps she could find a book of recipes at the general store. Her confidence climbed back up a notch. A cookbook would solve all her problems. "How many people live on Sutton Island, and how far is it to town?"

Imogen glanced up. Her delicate eyebrows came together. "There is no town on Sutton Island."

Annie sat up, the blankets dropping away from her shoulders. "No town?" Her heart bumped an erratic beat.

"Annie, Sutton Island is uninhabited except for the people needed to man the light. My husband is the head keeper, Nick is first assistant, and Clyde Moore is the second assistant. Then there's you and I. That's all."

Her mind froze. Five people. No stores, no church, no neighborhoods. No roads, no sidewalks, no milk delivery to the door. What had she gotten herself into?

"Didn't the inspector tell you when you applied for the

job? We're eight miles off shore. Halfway between Two Harbors and Split Rock where they're slated to build a lighthouse. The closest town of any size is Duluth." Imogen picked up her tatting again, but an arrow of concern remained between her brows. "You'll get used to it. Supplies are delivered by one of the lighthouse tenders, on either the *Marigold* or the *Amaranth*, though if there is a passenger to be dropped off at the island the *Jenny Klamath* will stop. If we need the ferry to pull in for some reason, we run a flag up at the end of the dock to let her know. And there's always plenty to do here. I never seem to get it all done."

Annie threaded her fingers through her hair to aid the drying. Five people, miles from any town. She, who had never lived outside Duluth, now perched on a rocky island in the middle of Lake Superior. Still, it might not be so bad. Her father would never think to look for her here, and the chances of running into someone who would recognize her were on the slim side.

"I think you should spend the rest of the afternoon in bed. We don't want you coming down with a cold. I thought I heard Clyde taking your trunk upstairs." Imogen tucked her handwork into a basket beside her chair. "I'll feed the men tonight and bring you up a supper tray. You can start your duties by cooking breakfast in the morning. The men like to eat at seven."

Breakfast for five people by seven tomorrow morning. Annie gathered her blankets and trekked up the narrow stairway. She'd have to come up with a plan, for to admit she couldn't cook would invite Imogen to send her packing back to Duluth and her father. Surely breakfast couldn't be that hard. . . .

❧

Nick tucked his hands behind his head and stared at the ceiling. A shaft of light raced across the room. He'd grown used to it by now, but the first few days had driven him nearly mad. The thin curtains did little to filter the powerful beam. He'd best close the blind if he wanted to get any sleep before his shift started at two. The green shade rattled down, blocking most of the light. At regular intervals, a white frame showed around the fabric then vanished.

His body ached, both from his lifesaving gambit this afternoon and from returning to the dock to help Clyde stow the boat. The girl invaded his thoughts. He scowled in the darkness then winced as his eye stung. She'd nailed him with her elbow. Good thing she hadn't knocked him out with the blow or they'd both have gone down to feed the fishes.

What was a girl like that doing on Sutton Island? Seasick and unable to swim, and from the look of her, barely old enough to be on her own. What were her parents thinking to let her take such a remote job?

His split knuckle throbbed. Scrubbing his boots hadn't done his hand any favors. He still couldn't believe she'd been sick on him.

She wouldn't last, not here. He gave her two weeks, just until the ferry returned and they flagged it down to pick her up. She'd be waiting on the dock with her bags packed, if he was any judge.

That water sure had been cold. Cold like he hadn't felt since. . .

Sleep crept over him.

Wind shrieked through the broken window, carrying swirling snow and icy pellets of spray. The captain huddled shoulder to shoulder with his men in the cramped pilothouse. The storm surge slammed the side of the ship, rolling her, pounding her against the shoal.

He lurched, his ribs throbbing, inhaling daggers with each breath. He'd lost feeling in his feet long ago, and now the cold crept up his legs. He shivered, ice hanging on his eyebrows and lashes, his breath a frosty plume that rimed his collar. Would the storm never end?

Then the deck heaved beneath his feet as he picked his way over ice-encrusted hatches and lines to the stern, clinging to the rail while surf surged over the ship. Low clouds scudded across the sky, the wind blowing them back out on the lake after the receding storm. He had to get to his crew in the stern. They would be all right if he could just get to them in time.

The men clung together, tied to the deck to keep from being swept overboard. The man nearest him had his face covered with his coat. The captain's hand trembled, but he forced himself to look.

He recoiled in horror. It wasn't a crewman. His brother's face, encased in a blue-white pallor, stared blankly up at him, frozen to death. His gaze darted from one face to the next. Jonathan. . .every face was Jonathan's. Dead, frozen, killed by his own brother's careless stupidity.

"Murderer!"

"Killer!"

"Coward!"

The accusations came from everywhere, hurled at him on the wind like shards of glass, slicing, ripping, shredding his soul. A mighty wave swept over the broken vessel, dousing him in frigid water, sweeping the bodies toward the rail.

"No, Jonathan, I'm so sorry. Please forgive me! Jonathan!" He tried to hang on to the body nearest him, but the lake pulled and sucked, tearing in a relentless battle until he lost his tenuous grip on Jonathan's sleeve.

"Jonathan!" He clawed and kicked, trying to swim in the icy waves, trying to grab Jonathan before he was towed under by the lake.

A giant seagull flapped over him, cawing and beating its wings. A blast of light hit his face, blinding him.

Nick woke, gasping, bathed in sweat. His heart bucked and surged. The window shade had snapped up, the cord and ring still swaying against the window. Another shaft of light coated the room and was gone.

The nightmare. Always the same, always horrible, always leaving him wrung out and exhausted.

He sat up and rubbed his hand down his face. Several deep breaths later, he assured himself that the dream wasn't real, that he hadn't killed his own brother. Jonathan was very much alive, probably at Kennebrae House sleeping beside his bride, Melissa, at this moment.

Nick swung his feet out of bed. He might as well relieve Ezra at the light. When the nightmare hit, there was no going back to sleep. As long as he was at the lighthouse, he was Nick, not Noah. If he worked hard enough, maybe he could forget.

five

Annie squinted at the kitchen clock and placed her hands at the small of her back, arching to stretch out the stiffness of a night in a strange bed. A yawn forced its way out, nearly cracking her jaw. Her eyelids sagged as if they had anchors attached to them. On a few occasions—first nights, galas, soirees, and such—she'd come home at this hour, but never had she risen from her bed so early.

The bacon sputtered and popped in the skillet. Annie poked the ragged strips with a fork. She had no idea how long to cook it. Just getting the stove lit had seemed a monumental task, the pungent odor of smoke still lingering in the air as a testament to the wisdom of opening the damper first thing.

"Good morning."

Annie whirled at the sound.

Mr. Batson, white shirtfront gleaming in the early morning light, stood in the doorway.

"Good morning . . .sir," she remembered to add.

"Imogen won't be down for breakfast, I'm afraid. She's feeling a bit under the weather. All the excitement yesterday, no doubt." He fingered his tie, as if checking that all was in order. "Clyde should be here soon, and Nick. Nick had the early-morning watch."

She nodded, her middle flopping as if seagulls were fighting over a piece of bread inside her stomach. "Should I take a tray up to her?"

Mr. Batson nodded, and a rush of satisfaction bubbled through Annie. She'd said the right thing.

"Perhaps midmorning. And keep her in bed as long as

you can. She's worn herself out trying to get things ship-shape before Inspector Dillon shows up."

Inspector? The very thought made anxiety wriggle up her spine. *Please, Lord, let me figure out what I'm doing before You bring down inspectors.*

Steam spurted from the oatmeal pot, rattling the lid. A mist of sweat coated Annie's forehead when she checked the contents. The cereal popped and bubbled like the tar the workmen had used to patch a neighbor's roof last spring in Duluth. Was it supposed to be this thick? Her shoulder complained when she tried to stir the sticky mass.

The kitchen door opened and banged shut.

She dropped the lid from nervous fingers, and it bounced off the corner of the stove and clattered to the floor. Nick. She prayed he wouldn't bring up her seasickness or her sudden departure from the dock. If he did, she might just melt right through the floor. She would thank him eventually, but she wanted to do it without onlookers.

Nick didn't even glance her way. Instead, he removed his cap and hung it on a peg by the door. He scanned the kitchen, breathed deeply, and frowned, looking at the ceiling.

Annie followed his gaze. She chewed her lip in consternation. Scarves of smoke lingered near the crown molding, evidence of her fight with the stove and the first batch of bacon she'd burned. She lowered her eyes and went back to fretting about breakfast.

But Nick drew her attention without even trying, making her pulse speed up. His shoulders seemed so broad he must've had to turn to get in the door. While he exchanged good mornings with Mr. Batson, Annie studied him. Dark brows shaded deep blue eyes, eyes that seemed to hold a wealth of sorrow. His somber expression didn't keep him from being handsome though. If anything, it gave him an air of vulnerability that made Annie want to offer him solace. Had he suffered a heartbreak? Had he lost someone dear to him? She suddenly wanted to know all about this man who had saved her life.

His glance right into her eyes yanked her back from spinning fanciful yarns. She grasped for some cool aplomb but failed. Nothing witty came to mind to say, so she lifted a hand in a slight wave.

He tilted his head to the side and looked at the stove behind her, eyebrows raised.

Annie sucked in a deep breath then coughed as air caught in her throat.

His left eye bore the faint shadow of a bruise. With a rush, Annie remembered flailing at him in the water. She must've given him that shiner during the rescue. Embarrassment trickled from her crown to her heels.

A scorching odor wafted around her. The bacon! Annie pivoted back to the stove, greeted by spitting, snarling, smoking grease. The strips of meat lay stiff in the hot fat, coated with charred blackness. She'd ruined another batch. But there was no time to cook more.

Chairs scraped behind her. She caught sight of Clyde sliding into his seat at the table, his hair sleep-tousled.

She plunked the meat onto a platter, wincing as hot bacon grease hit the top of her thumb. Good thing she'd set the table when she'd first come down. If they were going to be this prompt for breakfast, she might have to get up even earlier. The oatmeal defied her attempts to get it out of the pot, sticking like concrete to the metal. She finally tossed a trivet on the tablecloth, grabbed two cloths, and horsed the heavy pot to the table. They could serve themselves.

When everyone was seated, Mr. Batson bowed his head. "Almighty God, we thank You for Your bounty. Make us worthy. Amen."

Annie clenched her fists in her lap. *And please don't let anyone die from my cooking.*

Mr. Batson cleared his throat, and Annie looked up. He

lifted a strip of bacon onto his plate, frowning.

Clyde reached for the spoon sticking out of the oatmeal. He tugged, but when the spoon wouldn't budge, he let go, his eyes wide. He shot a look at Nick, who shrugged. "This cereal's sure"—Clyde scratched the hair over his right ear— "hearty." He smiled, as if relieved to have come up with a good word.

Nick grabbed the serving spoon and wrenched out a hunk of doughy oatmeal. The gray material defied gravity, clinging to the spoon, refusing to drop into his bowl—not even when he held it upside down and whacked the heel of his hand against the table to jar the oatmeal loose.

Annie closed her eyes. Humiliation coursed up her neck, through her cheeks, and into her ears. It prickled across her chest. She opened her eyes in time to see Clyde cover his mouth with his hand and shoot Nick a sympathetic look. Her chin went up. Who did they think they were, laughing at her?

"What did you say this was again?" Nick picked up his fork and scraped the cereal off the serving spoon and into his bowl. It landed without changing shape.

She shifted in her chair, wringing the life out of her napkin. "It's oat–meal." She enunciated each syllable.

"Hmm." He poked the mass with his fork. "I'll have to take your word for it."

Clyde snickered then wrestled his own spoonful of oatmeal. "Sure wish we had some fresh milk to thin this out a bit."

Annie sat helpless. So far, no one had braved to taste the food.

Mr. Batson touched his fork to a slice of bacon and it cracked into black bits.

She supposed she would have to be the first to eat a bite. When she lifted her bowl, Nick obliged her by dumping a spoonful of cereal in. Her arm wobbled at the unexpected weight.

She took her fork, licked her dry lips, and pried off a hunk of cereal. She put it in her mouth and was immediately reminded of damp newspaper and glue.

She chewed, keeping a pleasant expression on her face. Her hand gripped her water glass, and she took several big swallows to get the horrid stuff down. "Mmm. Just like home." She stared Nick in the eye, daring him to contradict her.

Clyde sniffed his before he put it in his mouth. He, too, must've needed water to coax it down his throat. "Ma'am, if this is what you ate at home, I have to say, I'm impressed."

As if on cue, all three men pushed back their plates. Annie tried not to look at their stares at one another.

"I guess we're not all that hungry this morning." Mr. Batson smoothed his already smooth shirt. "Don't forget to check on Imogen." His eyes twinkled. "And I don't believe she's hungry this morning either. Just tea should do her until she can come downstairs." He went into his office and shut the door.

Nick headed toward the porch, pushing Clyde before him. Annie couldn't help but notice both men take an apple from the bowl on the table by the door.

She hung her head. She'd be lucky if they didn't put her off the island at the first opportunity. Then what would she do?

"Lord, why aren't You helping me? Are You even listening? I can't do this by myself."

She clacked knives and forks together, scraping everything into the heavy pot of oatmeal to dump into the lake later. Plates clattered into the washtub. With a guilty start she remembered Imogen trying to rest upstairs. Poor lady. At least she'd missed having to eat breakfast.

A smile tugged at Annie's lips. Maybe God had answered one of her prayers. No one had actually died from eating her cooking. At least not yet.

Nick wrinkled his nose at the pungent smell of vinegar. He dampened the cloth and rubbed a spot on the window.

Waves crashed against the rocks over one hundred feet below, an incessant accompaniment, especially loud when, as now, the wind from the north pounded the waves into the caves just at the waterline. The Sutton Island Light perched on the edge of the cliff, embedded in the rock, as solid as the cliff itself.

Nick gripped the black rail of the catwalk with one hand and bent to the bucket at his feet. He enjoyed his task of washing the windows every day, inside and out, as well as wiping down the prisms of the clamshell Fresnel lens; but he would be glad when warmer weather came along. His hands, chapped by the vinegar and the wind, stung in the cold.

The glass gleamed, throwing back the sunlight. Rainbows ran along the curved prisms surrounding the kerosene lantern inside.

A sense of satisfaction settled over Nick. How quickly he'd dropped into his new routine. Familiar with the discipline of being a captain, the many regulations and duties of keeping a lighthouse didn't chafe him as they did Clyde. Nick's shoulder ached pleasantly from the scrubbing, and he dropped the rag in the bucket with a *plop*. Never again would he underestimate the efforts of his ship's crew when they swabbed the deck.

Nick brought himself up short. That all belonged to his past life. He narrowed his eyes and forced the thoughts aside. His life was here now, where he couldn't hurt anyone.

Several gulls shot up from the cliff face, squabbling and circling, pulling his attention away from the past. Noisy, messy birds, but as familiar to him as the waves lapping the shore.

A flash of gold caught his eye. Sunlight glinted off hair the color of ripe wheat. Miss Annie Fairfax. She lugged a bucket toward the edge of the cliff, the birds swooping and darting overhead. What was she doing? The rocky edge was stable, but the winds could be tricky. She should be more careful.

He ducked through the open window into the lantern deck, set the vinegar solution on the floor, and all but sprinted down the spiral staircase, through the watch room, and out into the sunshine. "Miss Fairfax," he called to her above the sound of the gulls diving on the contents of the bucket as he crossed the open space.

She gave a guilty start, lowering the pail.

The birds pecked at the gray lumps on the ground, flapping and hopping. They stole bits from each other, dropped them, and attacked the oatmeal again. Poor birds were in for a bit of indigestion.

"You shouldn't be so close to the edge." Nick took her elbow and guided her back a few steps. "We don't want you taking another tumble into the lake. I might not be able to fish you out from up here."

Her cheeks reddened, and her eyelashes fell to cover her surprisingly dark eyes. What an odd combination with hair so fair. It caught the light and threw it back, so shiny and bright. He'd never seen hair that color before. She wore it piled up, like one of those Gibson girl pictures. A few wisps touched her temples and cheeks, the breeze playing with the strands.

He realized he was staring and cleared his throat. "What are you doing up here?"

The tip of her tongue darted out to touch the corner of her mouth. "I was getting rid of the leftovers." She waved a hand toward the bucket.

"Ah, disposing of the evidence?" He cocked his head to one side. "I doubt the birds will thank you."

She dipped her chin, and he immediately regretted teasing her. Every cook could have a bad day, and the first attempt in a strange kitchen should be allowed some leeway.

No doubt lunch would be better.

Before he could apologize, she looked up. "I'll try not to kill the local fauna." She skewered him with a stare.

Hmm, not the delicate flower he first thought. She had some fight in her. And she looked so pretty all riled up he couldn't resist pushing her a bit further. "See that you don't kill the local human population either. And stay away from the cliff. I don't have time to keep an eye on you every minute of the day."

Her mouth dropped open.

A tingle of warmth raced through him at her hot glare.

"No one is asking you to." She bunched her skirts in one hand and stooped to pick up the bucket.

The gulls keened, swooping closer.

She turned away from the cliff and brushed past him.

Without thought, his hand jumped out and caught her arm. "Wait. Has anyone given you a tour of the buildings?"

"No, there's been no time." She tugged her elbow, trying to get away from him.

He tightened his grip. Why was he reluctant to part with her? "There's time now. You'll need to know what is safe and what isn't. Come, let me show you around." That was it. He was concerned for her safety.

Annie studied him out of the corner of her eye, her mouth pursed, her chin high. She looked like she would refuse him but finally said, "Very well."

An unreasonable happiness surged through him. What was the matter with him? He released her arm and took the bucket from her. "Let's start with the lighthouse."

She walked beside him to the red brick tower, looking up and blocking the sunlight with her hand.

"This lighthouse was built in 1899, so it's just seven years old. This little ell off the side of the tower is the watch room." He set the bucket down, held the door for her, and showed her through the sparse, tile-walled office that consisted of a plain desk, a wall lamp, and a small stove. They entered the tower, and he motioned for her to precede him up the shiny, black staircase. Their footsteps rang on the metal. The higher they climbed, the tighter the spiral, and the tighter her grip grew on the handrail.

They stepped into the lantern deck. Light shattered into a thousand rainbows through the prisms of the lens, dancing in the air, on her cheeks, in her eyes. Her hair glowed even brighter.

She sucked in a breath and laced her fingers together, tucking them under her chin. "It's so beautiful. Look how far you can see."

He followed her gaze across the cobalt water to the thin, white line of the horizon. Puffball clouds graced the pale sky. Foamy wave tips appeared and disappeared on the ever-moving lake. Far to the north, he could just make out the dark blot of a ship approaching. He turned to study Annie once more.

With her lips parted, eyes wide in wonder, she enchanted him. No one had ever affected him this way, making his heart thump faster, his palms sweat. Her lips, rosy pink, smiled at the vista before her.

Reality nudged him. *Kill those thoughts, buddy. There's no way she'd ever fall for you. If she knew the real you, she'd despise you.*

He turned his back to her. "This is a third-order Fresnel lens made in Paris with an incandescent oil-vapor lamp. Its official range is twenty-two miles. It gives a half-second flash every ten seconds." Much better. Keep the conversation on facts. He clasped his hands behind his back, staring at the top of the light above his head.

"It's quite impressive."

"I clean the windows every morning, wipe down the prisms, and trim the wicks, ready for lighting at dusk. According to the manual, the light must be completely ready for service by 10:00 a.m."

"Do you always follow the manual?" She held his gaze. "I can see the need for it, but don't you tire of the rigidity? The monotony?"

"No. I used to think life was no fun if you didn't take some risks, but I've learned better. The rules are there for a reason. They make the choices for you so you don't make mistakes that can be costly. There's safety in following routine. Without rules, you have disorder, chaos, and unnecessary risk." He crossed his arms and leaned against the window.

She shrugged, curling a tendril of hair around her slender finger. "I suppose, but if you only live inside the rules, there's no spontaneity. And you miss an awful lot of adventure."

"Adventure isn't all it's cracked up to be. Even if you do everything right it can still end badly, but doing things spontaneously always leads to disaster."

She regarded him skeptically and with what he thought might be a tinge of pity. He put it down to her age and inexperience. She'd soon learn how hard life could be.

"Let me go down the stairs first. That way, if you stumble, I'll be able to stop you from going all the way to the bottom." He started down the steps before her, listening to the *clang* of her shoes on each tread. They emerged into the sunshine once more.

"In addition to the lighthouse tower, there are four buildings on the island." He motioned to the two-story dwelling sitting at the foot of the lighthouse, the same red brick construction. "The main house, as you know, is for the head keeper and his family. Then there's the fog-house. A gasoline engine drives the air compressor that sounds the horn. We have to use it pretty often. The fogs can be bad on the lake."

They walked across the open space on a gravel path as he pointed out the various buildings and what role each played in the daily operations. He surprised himself at how much he was talking. He hadn't said so much to anyone since he'd been here, mostly preferring to work alone and retire to his room to read rather than socialize. But with Annie, he found himself more at ease than he'd been since arriving on the island.

They turned at the sound of a screen door slapping shut. Clyde jumped off the porch of the little house, a ladder over his shoulder, a paint can dangling from one hand. He lifted his chin in greeting, sauntering to a square wooden building set apart from the brick structures. He leaned the ladder against the eave and bent to open the paint. With broad strokes, he began painting another coat of white to the already-gleaming siding.

"What's that building then?" Annie waved toward Clyde.

"That's the fuel store. It's full of kerosene for the lighthouse and gasoline for the engines in the fog-house. You won't need to go in there. Just tell me or Clyde if you need kerosene for the house lamps and we'll get it for you."

She crossed her arms at her waist, the ties of her apron fluttering behind her. "I had no idea Sutton Island would be so isolated. Odd to think there's not another person for miles. It's disconcerting."

Nick rubbed his chin. The isolation didn't bother him. In fact, it suited him just fine, but it was a good reminder as to why he should steer clear of any entanglements with Annie Fairfax. No man with a past like his had any business getting mixed up with a girl like her.

She studied the horseshoe-shaped clearing then turned to look him in the eye. "I haven't had a chance to thank you properly for saving my life. And I'm sorry for being sick on the dock." Her delicate ears reddened, and her gaze dropped.

Uncomfortable, both with being thanked for something he'd done instinctively and with the protective feelings expanding in his chest, he shrugged and half turned away from her. "Don't mention it." He waved away her thanks. "You've seen the most dangerous places on the island. Stay away from the cliff, the fuel stores, and the tower. And it's against the rules for you to enter the lighthouse without one of the keepers. That should keep you safe. And considering the state of this morning's breakfast, I'll stay away from the kitchen. That should keep *me* safe." He grinned, waiting to hear her laugh.

She gasped, dropped her arms to her sides, and stalked off toward the house.

So much for his attempt at humor.

six

Pique carried Annie through heating water and preparing a tray for Imogen. High-and-mighty Nick Kennedy. See if she ever thanked him again. She threw teaspoons onto the tray more forcefully than she'd intended.

Still, it had been a little funny. Annie shook her head, smiling. The oatmeal had been truly awful. And the bacon . . .well, the bacon was best forgotten.

She carried the tray up the stairs, glancing out the window on the landing. Nick stood at the base of Clyde's ladder, speaking up to him. Interest and indignation battled within her.

"Come in," Imogen answered Annie's knock.

Annie backed into the room, trying to keep the tray steady. "Good morning. Mr. Batson thought you might like a cup of tea."

The room lay in dusk, light forcing its way around the edges of the dark shade. Imogen struggled up onto her elbows, her white hair lying over her shoulder in a narrow braid. "Aren't you a dear?" She patted her nightcap and tweaked the covers. Imogen's voice trembled a bit, sounding exhausted, though she'd lain in bed most of the morning.

"Here, let me help you." Annie propped pillows behind Imogen's head and shoulders. Annie set the tray before Imogen then turned to open the blinds on the east-facing windows.

Morning sun illuminated the room. Bold colors galloped across the bed in cheerful blocks of quilt fabric. An overstuffed chair draped with a crocheted afghan in bright granny squares sat on a braided rag rug beside a square oak dresser.

Imogen poured her tea then held the cup to her nose,

49

breathing in the wisps of steam rising from the fragrant liquid. She blinked in the bright light, her forehead screwed up. "I'm sorry I couldn't be downstairs to help with your first meal here. My head, you see. Sometimes the pain just wears me down."

"Oh, does it still hurt? Should I close the blinds?" Annie twisted her hands in her apron.

"That's all right, dear. Ezra brought me a headache powder early this morning. That usually pushes the pain down enough to be bearable."

Annie stood still for a moment then remembered her place in the household. She gave a quick nod to the mistress and started for the door.

Imogen's voice halted her. "I know you're busy, but please, sit down and visit with me a moment. There are a few things we need to talk about."

Apprehension quickened Annie's breathing. Had Imogen learned of the breakfast debacle? The guilt of her subterfuge—she balked at calling it outright lying—weighed in her chest like a lump of her own oatmeal. When she tried to perch on the edge of the upholstered chair, the squishy cushion gave way until she feared she might be swallowed.

Imogen set her teacup on the tray and regarded Annie with sober, dark eyes. She had such a look of patient strength, of serenity hard won through adversity, of total honesty, Annie wanted to squirm. "Tell me about yourself. I'm curious how you came to be in the Lighthouse Board's employ."

Surprised at not being chastised, Annie smiled. Then she realized what a giant pit yawned in front of her. Time to choose her words carefully. She didn't want to mislead this kind woman any more than she already had, especially when she was obviously suffering, but Annie also couldn't afford for the truth to come out. The Lighthouse Board would fire her and promptly pack her back to her father.

She cleared her throat, her mind racing. "My father works the mines up on the Mesabi mostly, though sometimes on the Vermillion." Well, that was true enough. He did own three mines, two on the Mesabi Iron Range and a smaller one on the Vermillion Range. "My mother passed away when I was young."

"So you grew up in a mining camp?" Imogen smoothed the edge of the blanket. "You've got very refined manners for being brought up by a miner. Or did your father remarry?" The question hung in the air between them.

Annie frowned. She'd never even seen one of the mining camps. Her father refused to take her up onto the range. She'd only be in his way. And the range was no place for a proper young lady. "My father never remarried. He left me in the care of a kind woman in Duluth. Now that I'm grown up, I need to be making my own way in the world. I saw an advertisement in the Duluth papers for a housekeeper and companion and applied." She kept her head down, her eyes on her hands in her lap. "The Lighthouse Board notified me by telegram that I had obtained the position, and here I am." She shrugged.

"Was there no young man set on winning your affection? Surely a girl as pretty as you would have her pick of suitors in Duluth?"

Annie heard again the muffled voices of her father and that old man in the wheelchair, plotting, arguing, and ultimately putting a price on her future, building a matrimonial cage around her bar by bar. An uprush of honesty propelled the words from her throat. "My father had someone in mind, but I'm not ready to get married, especially to my father's idea of a good husband. I want to be free to choose my own way. If I get married, it will be to someone who has nothing in common with my father. I want someone who will love me enough to stay with me, not to be racing off to his job, putting money ahead of his family. I want someone who will understand that people make mistakes, that they deserve forgiveness and second chances. I want someone who will love me first, last, and always. I won't be someone's second best."

She stopped, shocked at how much had poured out. She took a ragged breath and tried to smile to lessen the force of her words. "I'm sorry. I got a little carried away."

Imogen nodded, her lips twitching. "Ezra wasn't my father's pick for me either. Papa had me paired up with a stuffy banker back in Detroit. But I knew my future lay with Ezra from the moment I first saw him."

Annie tried to picture a young Ezra and Imogen falling in love. One look at Imogen's face made the picture easy to see. Love shone in every wrinkle, line, and tremble of the older woman's face. Her eyes, so dark in her pale face, glowed. Even with the headache dragging at her, she looked the part of a bride in love. Annie wondered if she would ever look that way when she spoke of a man.

"I have to ask how breakfast went. I thought I caught the scent of scorched bacon drifting up the stairs this morning. Was the stove giving you trouble? It can be such a beast sometimes."

Annie closed her eyes and lifted her chin. There was no way she could hide her lack of experience from this kind woman. "The stove was the least of my worries. Breakfast was a disaster. I burned two batches of bacon, and something happened to the oatmeal to make it suitable for chinking a log cabin. The truth is I haven't a clue how to cook. I can just about boil water for tea, but that's it." Her shoulders drooped, and a lump formed in her throat, cutting off her words. She was about to be fired, and she hadn't even held this job for twenty-four hours.

Imogen's soft laughter made Annie look up, blinking the moisture from her eyes. "Oh, Annie, I think you and I are going to get along just fine. When Ezra and I took our first lighthouse appointment, I couldn't cook either." The tray shook. "I burned a batch of biscuits so bad they turned to ash when I touched them. Took me a week to get the smoke smell out of the kitchen."

Tensed muscles relaxed, and Annie sagged against the back of the chair. She joined in the laughter weakly, strength drained from her for the moment. She never knew how exhausting relief could be.

Imogen put her hands on the sides of the tray to lift it away, but Annie struggled up from the chair. "Let me."

Imogen smiled up at her. "Don't you worry. I'll help. We'll have you as proficient as a sea cook in no time."

Before Annie could thank Imogen, a strange sound, like the buzzing of a hornet, filled the room.

"Oh no." Imogen halted halfway out of bed. "That's the *Marigold*'s ship horn. The inspector is on his way."

seven

Nick raised his head from the logbook and looked out one of the watch room's diamond-paned windows. Was that a ship's horn? He grabbed the field glasses from the window ledge and headed outside. A plume of smoke rose from a small ship to the north.

Ezra barreled around the corner.

Nick sidestepped at the last instant to avoid a collision.

"Follow me." Ezra hurried down the path toward the house.

"There's no fog." Nick easily kept up with the older man. "Is there a ship in trouble?"

"No, but we are. The captain of the *Marigold* and I have a little deal worked out. If the inspector is aboard the tender, the captain gives me a double blast of the ship's horn. We'll have about twenty minutes before Dillon sets out on the launch. I have to meet him at the dock."

Nick's heart rate increased. "What do you want me to do?" He tightened his grip on the field glasses.

"Go get into your uniform and make sure it's done up as per regulations. Then check that everything is ready in the tower. If you get time, stick your head in the fog-house for a quick look-see. I'll head for the dock to meet Dillon. And find Clyde. He was supposed to finish painting the fuel house. If he isn't there, he's probably down at the dock. I told him to haul the rowboat out and start painting it. He'll be needed to unload supplies." The last words floated over Ezra's shoulder as he disappeared into the house.

Nick jogged to his quarters, grimacing. Enough had been said about inspections to make him dread this one. He leaped onto the porch and hurried into the assistant keepers' house. Though it was dark, he wasted no time on raising the blinds. Two crates sat in the small front room. With the tender's arrival, more supplies would crowd the space by nightfall.

His own quarters, square, stark, and cleaner than a silver spoon at Kennebrae House, pleased him. He shucked out of his shirt and opened the locker at the foot of his bed. His uniform, purchased at his own expense, lay still wrapped in the brown paper the shopkeeper had tied it up in. When he'd asked Ezra upon arriving, his boss had said ordinary work clothes would suffice and to save the uniform for the inspector. Nick ripped off the paper and lifted the navy jacket out. A pang shot through his heart. The coat resembled his captain's uniform with bright brass buttons and a bit of gold braid on the lapels.

A snowy white shirt with new celluloid collar lay in the top drawer of the bureau. He donned it, tucking it in, grimacing at the tightness around his neck. He knotted the black tie at his throat then shrugged into the jacket.

The clock on the bedside table ticked away the seconds. Nick ran through his list of morning chores. He could think of nothing he'd failed to do.

He took his hat from the locker and placed it on his head, glancing in the mirror to make sure it sat at the proper angle. The collar pinched, and he dug his finger under it, tugging. His heart thumped.

Nick shook his head. It annoyed him that the arrival of one man could throw the entire complement of keepers into such a fuss. He understood about maintaining standards and ensuring the working order and operation of government property, but from the level of anxiety produced, it was as if President Teddy Roosevelt himself was arriving at the dock.

He stepped out of the house into the sunshine, shooting

his cuffs and picking a stray string from his jacket front.

"*Wooeee*, if you don't clean up nice." Clyde leaned the ladder against the porch rail and propped his elbow on one rung. "Did you hear that ship's horn?"

"Get that ladder out of sight and change your clothes. Then head to the dock to help unload supplies." Nick snapped out orders as to a crewman. "Inspector Dillon is arriving in a few minutes."

Clyde's eyes went wide, his pepper-pot freckles standing out in his pale face. He scooped up the ladder and paint can and disappeared.

Nick checked the watch room and the tower and took a quick glance into the fog-house as instructed. Everything looked shipshape. He took a deep breath then headed to the dock to support Ezra.

The *Marigold* rounded the north end of the island. Nick stepped onto the dock. Waves surged along the base of the cliff in restless, ceaseless movement. Within moments of dropping anchor, the steam-powered launch putted toward shore.

Clyde leaned against the cart, arms crossed, red hair blowing in the breeze.

Ezra paced the end of the dock, hands clasped behind him, head down. He snapped to attention when the boat bumped the pilings.

Nick caught the rope the deckhand tossed to him and made the launch fast.

Whatever Nick had expected Dillon to look like flew out of his head upon sight of the inspector. Jasper Dillon stepped over the gunwale and imposed his presence upon Sutton Island.

Nick topped him by at least ten inches. Even in his hat, Eleventh District Lighthouse Superintendent Jasper Dillon stood no more than five feet, two inches. Everything about the man was tiny, from his hands to his feet to his coal black eyes. If not for the hostile, defensive expression in those eyes, Nick might have been looking at a child.

Dillon made a sucking noise through his teeth, nodded to Nick and Clyde, and turned to Ezra. "Ah, Batson, I hope everything is in order?" He dug with slender fingers into his breast pocket and pulled out a toothpick. The wind fluttered the pages on the clipboard under his arm.

"Good to see you again, Inspector. I'm sure you'll find everything to standard."

Nick noted that neither man shook hands. With Dillon's ramrod posture and militant glare, perhaps a salute would have been in order.

Dillon whipped his head around to glare at Nick, almost as if he'd read Nick's mind. "You must be Kennedy." Dillon thrust his chin out, daring Nick to deny it.

"That's right." Something in him refused to cower or back down from this little bantam rooster. "I've heard a lot about you, sir." He deliberately let his tone indicate that not all he'd heard had been good. Nick was not accustomed to being talked down to, especially by a man who needed to look up to do it.

The inspector sucked hard through his teeth again, and the toothpick took a mauling. For a long moment he skewered Nick with his eyes. A smug smile tugged at his thin lips. "Mr. Kennedy, I should like you to accompany me on my inspection. Mr. Batson can oversee the unloading of the supplies." He lowered his clipboard and tapped his narrow thigh.

Ezra gave Nick a wide-eyed glance full of despair over Dillon's head. Nick nodded, as if Dillon's idea was the best he'd heard in a long time. "Right this way." He indicated the steep path up through the trees.

Dillon proved to be as demanding as Nick had been told. From the foundations to the roof vent, no surface in the tower went without scrutiny. The inspector ran his white glove over every sill, molding, and piece of furniture. Dillon got so close to the lens, his breath fogged the prisms.

Nick resisted the urge to sigh. He'd be the one to have to polish them again.

The fuel house received the same treatment, each barrel and container of fuel accounted for. This didn't take long as the bulk of their summer supplies was even now being unloaded on the dock. The only fuel in the place was that dropped off by the *Jenny Klamath* when Nick and the Batsons had arrived to open the light for the season two weeks ago.

Clyde arrived with the first load of kerosene drums from the shore just as Dillon started toward the fog-house. Clyde gave Nick an impudent grin behind the inspector's back.

Nick averted his face to keep from laughing aloud.

In the fog-house, Dillon went over every inch of the gasoline engines, making marks on his clipboard, sucking on his teeth. Through it all, Nick stood silent by the door. Dillon would find nothing amiss. Everything, from the shingles to the doorsill, was exactly as prescribed in the manual.

Thank You, Lord, for Ezra Batson and his insistence on everything being by the book.

Dillon's mouth twisted in a persimmon pucker. "I should like to inventory the tools now." He sucked in a giant breath that moved his shirtfront only a little. A solid gust of wind would sweep the man right over the cliff face.

"Tools are kept in the assistants' quarters. Right this way."

"Fine. I'll come back for the house inspection."

They crossed the clearing, Nick careful to keep pace with the inspector. He refused to walk behind the pompous little man.

They passed the front porch of Ezra's house. From within, a pot clanged against metal and a mutter followed. He shrugged away his unease. Surely Annie would have everything under control there.

❧

Annie scrunched her eyes up tight and sucked on her

throbbing finger. In her haste to get the dirty dishes out of sight, she'd pinched her finger in a door. Hot tears smarted at the corners of her eyes, but she blinked them away. There was no time to cry.

She wrestled with the window over the sink, trying to get it open to rid the kitchen of the stale smoky smell. Slow footsteps overhead indicated Imogen moving about, no doubt dressing and putting up her hair.

Her hair! Annie's hands flew to her straggling bun. Being outside in the wind had tousled it, and tearing about the house hadn't improved the job. At least this was one task she was comfortable with. Though Hazel had usually done Annie's hair for going out, Annie had enjoyed styling her own hair most days.

She sped up the stairs to her bedroom and grabbed her hairbrush from the dresser. The pins snarled in her hair, her fingers clumsy in haste. She brushed it then began the process of winding it up into a perfectly relaxed knot. She winced when a hairpin jabbed her scalp, but in moments every lock was in place.

Looking behind her in the mirror, she screwed up her face at the mess. Never having had to care for her own belongings, she had scattered possessions hither and yon last night and this morning in her search for a suitable outfit. Good thing the inspector wasn't likely to come up here. The very idea of a strange man invading a girl's sleeping quarters!

Imogen met her in the hall, her face pale, her fingers chilly when she grabbed Annie's hands. "Did you get the kitchen squared away?"

"There wasn't much time. I did the best I could." Annie helped Imogen down the stairs. "You should've stayed in bed."

"I'll be fine. I'll sit in the parlor. You'll have to be in the kitchen, but don't say much. Dillon doesn't like back talk, and he won't overlook anything."

"I'll hold my tongue." Even as she said it, Annie wondered if she could. She wasn't accustomed to stifling her words.

Annie got Imogen settled on the sofa and went into the kitchen. She arrived none too soon.

Nick held the door open to allow a small man to precede him inside. "This is Inspector Dillon. Inspector, Miss Fairfax." Nick stepped inside and leaned against the wall beside the door. He crossed his arms, his face impassive.

A shiver raced across Annie's shoulders at the intense way Nick's eyes bored into hers. She licked her lips, and when he gave her a quick wink, she giggled.

"Madam? You find something amusing?" The inspector crossed his wrists behind his back and rocked heel to toe, pausing on his forward movement momentarily, as if trying to make himself taller. He gave an obnoxious suck on his teeth, the air whistling in moistly. The clipboard stuck out from one hand.

"Ah, no, I'm sorry. Pleased to meet you, sir. Won't you make yourself comfortable? Would you like a cup of tea?" Annie winced at her rapid-fire words.

"No, thank you. This is not a social visit. Just keep out of my way."

Annie backed up until she ran into a counter. Her hands suddenly seemed to be too large and in the way. She put them behind her and gripped the rolled edge of the enamel sink.

"I'll start with the pantry. I'd like to see the inventory of goods." The inspector held out his hand, tapping his foot on the bare kitchen floor.

Annie shot a look at Nick who shrugged. She had no idea what the inspector wanted.

"Well? Where is it?"

"I. . .I. . ." She shook her head.

"Hmm." The clipboard came up and he dug a pencil from his pocket. "No inventory sheets."

Annie closed her eyes. Surely Imogen had them some-where. Her eyes shot open when the pantry door squeaked.

Dillon disappeared, and soon, the sounds of tins clanking, stone crocks scraping the floor, and glass tinkling filtered out.

Nick moved to her side. "Inventory sheets?"

Her heart accelerated at his closeness. He smelled of soap and lake breeze. "I haven't seen any. Do you suppose it's important?" Her voice rasped low. "How did the rest of the inspection go?"

"No idea. He doesn't say much, just barks his questions and orders and struts on." His voice held a laugh, and when she looked up into his eyes, he grinned at her.

Was it hot in here?

"I have a bad feeling about this. I've only been here one day. Surely he can't expect me to know where everything is. That's unreasonable."

"The inspector seems to deal in unreasonable." Nick straightened up.

Dillon emerged from the pantry, his mouth in a hard line. "Someone"—he glared at Annie—"spilled oatmeal on the floor. And there are several pots missing, as well as the washtub."

Annie gulped. Before she could speak, Dillon began yank-ing open cupboards and drawers. Cutlery clattered, wood scraped, and Annie's nerves stretched.

Please, please, please, God, if You're listening, don't let him—

Too late. The inspector opened the oven door. Annie grimaced. The dishpan, stacked high with dirty pots and dishes, cowered in the oven where she'd shoved it out of sight only a few minutes before.

"What is this?" Dillon puffed up with outrage. His small white forefinger pointed first to the dishes then to Annie. His chin lifted until he was staring down either side of his narrow nose.

Hot embarrassment shot through her. She looked at the

floor, not wanting to see Nick's reaction.

"Get these out of here." Dillon tapped his foot.

Annie stepped forward, but Nick put his hand on her arm. In two strides he crossed the kitchen and slid the washtub from the oven. Annie answered his inquiring look by nodding toward the counter beside her.

Dillon gave them each a sharp glare then pivoted on one heel and entered the parlor.

"Thank you." Annie choked on the whisper.

"You'd better follow him. I'll be out on the porch." His kind smile shot warmth through her that had nothing to do with embarrassment.

She found Dillon and Imogen in the front room. Imogen, though pale, held herself regally, the match of any inspector.

Dillon seemed to realize this, for he treated her with a deference that had been decidedly lacking in his behavior toward Annie. But his eyes never stopped moving, calculating, assessing. "I'll just check a few more things, Mrs. Batson, then the men will convene to the fog-house to discuss issues at this station." He bowed quickly then ducked out of the room.

"How did it go in the kitchen, dear?" Imogen laid her head back against the chair and sighed.

"He found where I'd stashed the dirty dishes." Annie spread her hands wide.

A soft chuckle escaped Imogen's lips. "You didn't put the dishes in the oven, did you? That's the first place they look."

Annie laughed ruefully in return. "I wish you'd have told me that sooner. I'd have hidden them in my room."

"They wouldn't be safe there either. He's checking the bedrooms right—"

"Miss Fairfax!" For such a little man, he had a loud voice.

Dread and hot anger gushed through Annie. She grabbed her skirts and hustled up the stairs. How dare he!

He stood in the doorway to her room, his face red, eyes

blazing hot enough to start a fire. "What is the meaning of this?" He held up one of her petticoats.

The sight of Dillon holding her undergarment knocked all sense of caution out of Annie. She snatched the item from his hand. "Sir, this station may belong to the Lighthouse Board, but the Board does not lay claim to my personal items. I will thank you to stop pawing through my possessions. It is unseemly." Annie stood to her full height, topping the inspector by several inches. She refused to cower, and she refused to allow him to push her around any longer, the picky prig.

His mouth gaped and his eyes glassed over until he resembled a fish fresh from the lake. His nostrils flared, a dull redness suffusing his cheeks.

Annie tightened her lips. She'd gone too far. Imogen had only asked that Annie hold her tongue, and what had Annie done? Lashed out like a cornered badger at the first opportunity. She waited for the hammer to fall, for Dillon to order her to gather her strewn belongings and get off his island.

They stood toe-to-toe for a moment longer. Then, to her surprise, Dillon whirled and stomped down the stairs without a word.

Annie walked on unsteady legs to the bed and sank down, causing the springs to squeak. Her heart thundered against her ribs and her breath came in quick pants. She'd faced him down, but now what? Would he write her up in some wretched report? She'd be lucky if he didn't send her packing on the next ferry south.

She looked about her room. Her traveling costume from the day before huddled in a damp and sorry heap where she'd stepped out of it. Petticoats and stockings snarled together in a pile beside her valise, which lay on its side open and spilling out her spare chemises and drawers. Her trunk stood open, a heap of clothing piled in the tray.

Heat scorched her face at the thought of any man, much less the insufferable inspector, seeing her possessions in such disarray. She rose and, for the first time in her life, began folding and putting away her own clothing.

eight

Dillon made his departure midafternoon. Though everyone but Imogen assembled on the dock to see him off, he spoke only to Mr. Batson.

Nick stood off to the side, watching, impatient for the inspector to be gone. The routine of Nick's day had been thrown awry, and he was anxious to get it back on track. And his stomach growled. He'd had nothing to eat since yesterday evening but an apple. Dillon had kept them talking in the fog-house through the lunch hour.

He wondered how things in the house had gone after he left. Annie stood at the head of the dock, not venturing out over the water, her hands clenched at her waist, the wind blowing her skirt and hair. She didn't look at Dillon, or anyone else for that matter. A thrust of pity for her jabbed him. She was too young, too green for this job. What had driven her to take this position, so obviously wrong for her?

Dillon's nasal voice punched into his thoughts. "The lighthouse, fog-house, and fuel stores are all in fine condition. I commend you on their orderliness and cleanliness." He rocked on his toes, mauling another toothpick in his teeth. "The buildings and grounds are in excellent condition, better than I had expected considering how early in the season it is."

Clyde shot Nick an eyebrow-wobbly look, grinning through his freckles. The kid had a reckless zest for life that made Nick smile. Oh to be that naive again, to roll through life with few cares, little baggage, and a sense of adventure.

"However," Dillon went on, "the domestic side of things is another matter altogether. The kitchen, pantry, and sleeping quarters were disastrous."

Nick glanced at Annie. She winced, seeming to shrink a little with each barb. He had a sudden urge to go to her, to put his arm around her and tell her it would be all right. Where had that come from? She was nothing to him. Why then did he have the desire to shove his fist through Dillon's face for upsetting her?

"Because housekeepers are so difficult to obtain for remote stations such as Sutton Island, I am not going to fire Miss Fairfax at this time, no matter how much she may deserve it. Mrs. Batson tells me she is satisfied with Miss Fairfax's work, though I don't know how she could be. No, I'm not going to fire Miss Fairfax, but I am putting her on notice. I will return to inspect the station again, and if I find anything out of place, her employment will be terminated. From this moment on, Miss Fairfax is on probation. And while she is on probation, I will be looking for another candidate to fill her position. Should a suitable housekeeper apply, I will replace Miss Fairfax. Is that understood?" He tossed his toothpick onto the dock and dug in his pocket for another. The breeze flapped the papers on his ever-present clipboard, and Nick imagined himself ripping the clipboard from Dillon's hands and tossing it into the lake.

Ezra nodded, eyes sober, glancing between Dillon and Annie. "I understand. Thank you, Inspector. Are you sure you won't stay for some lunch?"

Nick looked heavenward. That was tempting things. If Annie cooked him a lunch anything like her breakfast, Dillon might set her adrift in a rowboat to find her own way back to Duluth.

"No, no, not this time. I can still inspect Two Harbors if I leave now. Good day, Batson, and don't forget what I said about a new housekeeper." Dillon clambered aboard the launch, sat stiffly upright in the bow, and pointed his face toward the *Marigold* lying at anchor a few hundred yards offshore. The launch puttered away, plowing through the waves, taking the inspector to wreak havoc elsewhere.

Nick laughed when he realized everyone on the dock had let out a big sigh of relief.

Ezra's mouth twisted in a wry smile. "I always look forward to that man's departure."

"What a way to live." Clyde hopped up onto a barrel of kerosene and gently drummed his heels against the metal side. "Folks never glad to see you come, always happy to see the back of you. What makes him so disagreeable?"

Nick unbuttoned his heavy wool tunic and slid out of the sleeves. Ezra did the same, and removed his hat as well.

"I try to be a little more understanding of him than most, I suppose." Ezra threaded his fingers through his flattened hair. "I met him once in Duluth, with his wife. She must be twice his size and has the disposition of a mule with a toothache. That man is oppressed, henpecked, and altogether dominated at home. I suppose he had to exert his will somewhere, and he takes it out on the folks in his employ."

Nick tried to imagine Dillon's domestic situation. It boggled the mind.

"I'd be nicer to people then, if it was me." Clyde hunched his shoulders. "'Cause I would know how it felt to be bossed and pushed around."

"I think I would, too, though I can't see either of us as henpecked husbands." Ezra smiled. "Imogen isn't the bossy type, and I imagine you'd have more sense than to marry someone like Mrs. Dillon in the first place. How about we get these supplies up the hill and stowed away. . .according to regulations." The corners of his eyes crinkled in humor.

Nick tossed his coat over a crate and picked the box up to move it to the cart for transport up the hill. A tiny part of him felt sorry for the inspector, and a larger part felt grateful to have escaped the same fate himself. Who knew what kind of woman his grandfather had picked out for him? Just because she was the daughter of Grandfather's crony didn't mean she wasn't a shrew.

Annie still stood at the head of the dock, staring out over the water toward the *Marigold*. A sort of forlorn resignation rested on her pretty features, drawing down the corners of her eyes and mouth.

"Don't take it to heart, Annie. A few dishes in the oven aren't the end of the world."

She nodded, blinking her brown eyes hard a few times. A deep sigh escaped her lips as the lighthouse tender weighed anchor, gave a blast of the horn, and headed southwest to Two Harbors. "If that's all it was, I wouldn't be too worried. I lost my temper with him and made him look foolish." Her mouth quirked up. "Inquisitive, nosy, bothersome man. I wish he had stayed to lunch. I'd have fed him some of my oatmeal."

Nick laughed, surprised at her ability to joke about something that had angered her only a short while ago. Were all women this mercurial in temperament?

When he turned around from placing the crate on the cart, Annie was making her way up the footpath, occasionally glancing back over her shoulder toward the lake. Probably making sure the nasty little inspector wasn't returning.

"Clyde, head up the hill and light a bonfire. Throw some green leaves on it to make it smoke good." Ezra set two five-gallon containers of gasoline into the cart. "You can just see a good smoke column from here at Two Harbors. We'll try to warn them he's coming their way."

Clyde grinned. "Smoke signals. Great idea."

"Only fair. A little warning makes all the difference."

Nick slung the mailbag into the cart. A little warning. If he'd had a little warning about the storm last fall, he'd never have left the harbor. He wouldn't have been caught in the storm, and he wouldn't have found himself in the Lighthouse Board's employ, subservient to a tyrannical inspector.

Another glance up the hill. Sunlight gleamed off her golden hair. And he'd never have met a feisty girl named Annie Fairfax.

❧

Sunday dawned clear and bright. Imogen, feeling better this morning, gave Annie a cooking lesson. Pride glowed around Annie's heart when the men sat down to an edible meal for the first time since her foray into the culinary arts. Black frills decorated the edges of the fried ham, and the eggs were past hard, but the biscuits more than made up for any shortcomings. They were light, hot, and fluffy, just begging for honey.

When the dishes were cleared away—washed this time, not stuck in the oven—everyone gathered in the parlor for Sunday services. Annie entered the room last, her Bible clutched in her hand, to find the only available seat was on the davenport between Clyde and Nick. She sat between them, trying to make herself small so as not to touch either of them. Her shoulder brushed Nick's. She glanced up to see him staring down at her, intense and focused. Her mouth went dry, and she dropped her gaze to her Bible in her lap.

Ezra prayed. He spoke formally but as if he prayed often.

Annie wondered what it would've been like to grow up with a man like Ezra as her father.

"Our text for today is found in Proverbs 18:10. Nick, would you read that for us?"

Nick opened his Bible, the onion papers rustling like poplar leaves in a breeze. " 'The name of the Lord is a strong tower: the righteous runneth into it, and is safe.' "

"What does that mean to you?" Ezra looked at Clyde.

"We have a safe place to run when things get tough."

Annie froze, hoping Ezra wouldn't call on her for her opinion. She hadn't even opened her Bible. What did the verse say again? Her hands went cold.

"Annie?"

She shook her head, mind racing.

"That's all right. Nick?"

"We serve such a powerful God that even His name holds safety for us. He has promised never to leave us, and we know that if we are in trouble, He is waiting to help us. He won't abandon us."

Abandonment. Annie knew a thing or two about that. Maybe God didn't abandon good men like Nick or Clyde, or good people like the Batsons, but why hadn't He saved Neville? Why hadn't He stopped Mother from losing her reason or Father from shunning Annie after Neville died? Annie's thoughts whirled like a mini-tornado, memories and old hurts clashing with the words of the verse. *A strong tower. A strong tower.*

Ezra spoke again. "This promise is supported again and again in the Old Testament. I can believe this promise now because God kept His promises to the Israelites way back. Every time they called on Him, He heard them. He was a strong tower for them in their times of trouble. He never once left them, and He won't leave us either. All we have to do is run to Him. I take great comfort in that."

Imogen nodded, her face peaceful and loving, eyes intent on her husband.

Sure, she can agree with him. Ezra adores her. They've been together a long time. He's never abandoned her. Annie feared she would never know that closeness with anyone. Certainly not with someone her father chose for her out of greediness for money and power.

At Ezra's bidding, Clyde stood and picked up his guitar. With a nod to Imogen, he put his foot on the low table and settled the instrument on his knee. He strummed the strings, sending music vibrating through the room. In a clear tenor, he sang a few words of a familiar hymn.

Everyone joined in, Annie doing so automatically, though

her thoughts remained on the Bible verse and her reaction to it.

❧

Clyde opened the mailbag for everyone, a treat put off in the busyness of yesterday to be savored in the quiet of a Sunday afternoon.

Annie knew there would be nothing for her since she'd only just arrived at the island, though she couldn't help but catch some of the excitement from the others.

Clyde received a package and letter from his mother in Superior. "Socks. She knows me well." Clyde held up a handful of gray wool. "And Pa's got a new job at Kennebrae Shipping. He's working on the *Bethany*. Guess they were able to salvage her."

Nick had a letter he tucked into his pocket without reading. He must want privacy. Annie could appreciate that. Was it from a sweetheart at home? She couldn't tell. He didn't look particularly eager to read the letter, nor excited about the sender. Surely if it was from a girl, he'd be less grim.

She chided herself for being so inquisitive and turned her attention to Imogen. Imogen received two letters and Ezra one.

Then there were the papers. Everyone took a Duluth newspaper, regardless of the date, and began reading. Annie found herself looking at yesterday's paper. She smoothed the crisp pages in her lap then held them up to hide her smile. At home, Father never would've approved of Annie reading the newspaper. Such behavior was unbecoming to a lady. She wondered at how much her life had changed in just a single week. Washing dishes, folding clothes, sweeping floors, and now reading newspapers.

Annie's eyes finally focused on the article under the masthead:

LOCAL HEIRESS DISAPPEARS
Anastasia Fairfax Michaels, only daughter and heir

*to Phillip Michaels, was reported missing early Friday
morning. Phillip Michaels, owner of Michaels Mining and Manufacturing, reportedly worth more than
one hundred million dollars, told police early yesterday
morning that his daughter had disappeared from their
Skyline Parkway mansion. Anastasia (19), a recent
graduate of the Duluth Ladies' Academy, stands to
inherit the Michaels fortune someday. The family is
distraught. Michaels told this reporter his daughter was
betrothed to a prominent Duluth businessman, though
the formal announcement had yet to be made. Michaels
refused to give us the name of the groom-to-be at this
time.*

*Authorities are baffled by the case. So far, no ransom
demand has been made and no plausible theories as to how
a kidnap could have occurred have been put forth. Is this a
kidnapping? Or did the young lady elope?*

*When the possibility of his daughter's running away
was broached, Michaels became violently angry, shouting at reporters and police alike. "She wouldn't do anything so foolish. All her things are here, even her jewelry.
If she ran away, why didn't she take them with her? I
demand you find her and bring her back. I'll pay five
thousand dollars' reward to anyone who will help get my
daughter back." He then ordered his footmen to escort all
news personnel off his property.*

Annie glanced up.

No one looked at her. All were engrossed in their reading.

She stood. "I believe I'll take this upstairs to finish reading." Her pulse throbbed in her throat. The paper shook in
her hands.

She reached her bedroom and leaned against the closed
door. She quickly scanned the article again. Annie hadn't

thought about the press or the police when she'd fled, only escaping her father's marriage plans for her. Leaving everything behind and being outfitted by Hazel in ordinary clothes, not even writing a note to anyone, had all been necessary to her escape. Just getting away wouldn't have been enough. She had to get away without anyone knowing her whereabouts. Well, no one but Hazel, and she'd never tell.

That must be why Hazel hadn't told the police it wasn't a kidnapping. She could hardly say she knew Annie had fled without saying she also knew where Annie had gone. Anyway, Hazel was probably on her way to Hibbing to that retirement cottage promised to her by Father.

Father. Annie rolled her eyes. Just like him to demand people help him then throw them out. And she couldn't believe he'd mentioned the betrothal. How could he still be planning the wedding when she wasn't even there? "I bet if I showed up in Duluth today, he'd have me married by tomorrow."

Guilt gnawed at her for causing such a fuss. Surely all the uproar would die down in a week or so, wouldn't it? She folded the paper, wondering where to hide it. Another headline below the fold caught her eye. SALVAGE CONTINUES ON *KENNEBRAE BETHANY*." Evidently the *Bethany*'s captain had left Duluth. Poor fellow, she didn't blame him. Folks would be talking about the wreck of the *Bethany* for years to come. Annie finished the article and stuffed the paper into a drawer. She'd take it down to the kitchen before breakfast tomorrow and burn it. It just wouldn't do for anyone here to see it. They'd make the connection between Anastasia Fairfax Michaels and Annie Fairfax in two blasts of a foghorn.

nine

Nick pumped air into the fuel tanks to pressurize them to the proper level. He tested them, a fine mist of kerosene spraying out of the nozzle. Perfect. He shielded his eyes and lit the oil-vapor lamps inside the lens. The lantern deck burst into white hot light.

One last squinting glance around the edge of his hand to confirm all was well and Nick clanged down the spiral staircase to the bottom of the tower. He checked the chains in the column then wound them slowly and evenly, cranking at a steady pace to ensure they didn't tangle. He checked his watch then engaged the gears. The light above began to revolve. He watched for four complete revolutions, timing them with his pocket watch. Perfect, one flash every ten seconds.

The chair creaked familiarly beneath him. He scooted it up to the desk and reached for his pen to update the log.

> *Tanks pumped and lantern lit at 7:34. Chains wound and light timed. Weather clear, slight breeze from the northeast. Three ships sighted before dusk, one ore carrier and one lumber boat with hooker in tow. N. Kennebr—*

He stopped in frustration. He'd almost signed his real name. He dipped his pen into the ink and deliberately let a blob fall on his signature. Good thing he'd noticed his slip. Ezra might ask some awkward questions.

Rules dictated every action taken concerning the light be logged while on watch. Past logs entries made for some interesting reading. The first keeper here, a man named Orrin Olden, was particularly wordy. His entries spoke of bad weather, a ship just off the coast whose boiler exploded, causing the ship to go down so quickly the keeper didn't even have time to launch a rowboat to save anyone aboard. One entry told of a lightning storm over the island. Not even the lightning rods on the tower kept bolts from striking the buildings. Nick flipped back to that entry.

> *Terrible lightning storm last night. Windows broke in the tower, but the lens, thank the Lord, is still intact. Lightning shot out of the faucets and raced in fist-sized balls across the floor and into the parlor. By far the strangest oddity of the storm was the lard bucket I'd set beside the downspout on the corner of the house. When I looked at it this morning, it had hundreds of tiny holes pierced through it. Guess I won't be using that as my bait bucket anymore. —Orrin Olden.*

Nick flipped back to the current page and signed "Nick Kennedy" next to the ink blotch. He checked the wall clock, then his watch, then stepped outside.

Clyde sat on the back porch of the Batsons' house, strumming his guitar and singing. In the twilight, Nick picked out Annie's form leaning against a porch post, her hair pale in the growing dusk. Every ten seconds the soft edge-glow of the lighthouse's beam circled overhead, briefly illuminating the Batsons sitting on the porch swing.

An owl hooted in the trees behind the house, preparing for his night hunt. From below the cliff, a fish jumped, flopping into the water with a *smack*. Must have been a big one. Perhaps Nick could find a little time tomorrow to fish off the dock, though he wondered what Annie would do if he presented her with a half dozen fish to cook.

Had that last rotation of the light been slow? Nick counted, waiting for the next flash to hit the chimney of the house. Eleven. He'd better check. He was probably counting too fast.

He stepped into the tower and held his watch to the wall sconce. Eleven, almost twelve. A quick check told him the weights weren't fouled in the shaft nor were the cables tangled. The rotations continued, but each was just a few seconds slow.

Ezra arrived before Nick got halfway up the stairs. "Is the light slow?"

"Yes, I'm just headed up to check on the mechanism from up there." Nick shielded his eyes when he reached the lantern deck and ducked down to observe the clockworks at the base of the light. The hot smell of burning kerosene filled his nose. The heat generated by the lantern was intense, though much of it drifted up through the vent ball in the roof. He saw nothing wrong. The light hurt his eyes even though he tried not to look at it.

He rejoined Ezra in the watch room. "I can't tell. Everything seems to be running well. We won't be able to tear it apart and look at it until tomorrow." Nick blinked, still seeing spots.

Ezra stroked his chin. "We'll have to turn it by hand then. I'll get Clyde."

Nick rolled up his sleeves, turning back the cuffs in precise folds. It was going to be a long night. He looked up when Ezra returned with Clyde. Nick jumped to his feet when Annie entered the watch room.

Ezra crossed his arms. "I've decided we'll work in shifts. Nick, you'll take the first watch. Annie has volunteered to keep the time for you. We'll alternate two-hour watches until daylight. Annie"—he turned to her, handing her a marine stopwatch—"ten seconds exactly for each flash of the light, twenty for the clamshell to turn once around completely, right?"

She nodded, her dark eyes appearing black in the light from the wall sconce.

Ezra and Clyde left to try to get some sleep before their

watch, leaving Nick and Annie alone in the watch room.

Nick studied her then picked up the chair from the desk and took it into the tower. He set it along the wall under a lamp for her.

She wrapped her shawl tighter around her shoulders and sat down. "How do you want me to do this?" Two narrow vertical lines appeared between her eyebrows. Her bottom lip disappeared behind her upper teeth.

"Count out the seconds. You'll have to do it loud enough that I can hear. I'll be turning this crank." He motioned to the lever. "It's attached to the gears that turn the light."

"Why is it so important that the light flash at ten second intervals? What's wrong with eleven or twelve? Isn't the fact that the light is shining at all enough?"

Nick began the process of disengaging the chains and weights from the gears. "Every light on the lake has its own signal, its own timing, and its own color. Some of the lanterns are green, some are white, some are red. The precise timing of the light lets mariners know which light they are near. There's a whale of difference between, say, the lighthouse at Two Harbors and the lighthouse at Devil's Island. If the captain doesn't know or can't tell the difference, just having the light won't be enough to keep him from running aground if he thinks he is somewhere he's not. Even then, you can't always avert disaster. A lighthouse shouldn't give a captain a feeling of safety. It should increase his awareness of danger."

"It makes me think of all the ships that were lost last fall. Remember the *Bethany*? Her captain was within sight of the Duluth Harbor Light when he ran aground. All winter that ship sat there in the ice. I wonder what happened to that captain."

Nick bent to the lever without answering her. Guilt, shame, anger, everything he'd been trying to escape by coming to Sutton Island was trapped within his chest. "Start counting."

❧

"Four, five, six, seven, eight, nine, ten. One, two, three. . ." Annie continued to count aloud. Her tongue stuck to the roof of her mouth, and she longed for a cup of hot tea.

Nick bent over the crank, turning, turning, turning, never stopping. Sweat dripped from his forehead and patches soaked the back of his white shirt, sticking it to muscles that moved and rippled with each turn.

Annie tugged her shawl tighter around her shoulders and wiggled her toes in her boots. The temperature had dropped as the hours passed. Soon she would be able to see her breath. Sitting in a stone-and-iron tower during a Lake Superior April night was enough to bring on pneumonia.

"Six, seven, eight, nine, ten. One, two, three, four. . ." *This is how people go insane. Whoever says lighthouse keepers' jobs are easy is a fool.* They were on watch every hour of every day. What made them choose this work? They had to be men of extraordinary commitment. Men who wouldn't run away when things got tough. Not like her father—

She shut that line of thought down and concentrated on counting. And she watched Nick.

Nick would be a good husband. He was kind, honorable, and hardworking. He loved God and never shirked a duty. Imogen sang his praises, and Ezra and Clyde got along with him so well. And a girl would have to be blind not to see how handsome he was. His behavior toward Annie had been perfect. Well, except for a little teasing about her cooking, but only the once. Yes, he would be a good husband.

"Nine, ten. One, two. . ." Not like the worm her father had chosen for her. Annie envisioned a miserly, middle-aged grump with bad breath and thinning hair. He probably smoked foul-smelling cigars and maybe even wore a monocle. He'd drone on endlessly about capital ventures and voting shares when he bothered to speak to her at all. She would be expected to run his house smoothly, see to all his comforts, and, above all, produce an heir and preferably a spare within the first five years of marriage. As a proper wife, she would be required to attend such functions as he permitted and to overlook all his faults, particularly those involving breaking the seventh commandment. And he would magnanimously overlook her past sins so he could get his grubby mitts on her inheritance. Annie's fingers gripped the stopwatch so hard, her hand shook.

"Five, six, seven. . ." If her father had chosen a man like Nick instead of some spineless grub with dollar signs in his eyes, she never would've fled Michaelton House. But no man of Nick's fine character would want to be mixed up with someone like her, money or no money.

"We'll take over now." Annie looked up to see Clyde taking over the crank and Ezra reaching for the watch.

Annie handed it over and attempted to rise. Her muscles had stiffened in the cold and inactivity. Pain pressed into her lower back like pushpins. Her feet were blocks of ice.

Nick held out his hand to help her rise. "You look worn out. We'd best go get some sleep before we have to come back in a couple hours and do it all over again." He brushed a lock of hair off her cheek, the contact of his fingers on her skin sending spiraling jitters through her middle.

Her breath caught in her throat, and she told herself not to be silly, he was just being kind. She had let her imagination get away from her a bit, that was all. Her mouth trembled into a smile. "Good idea. I'll set my alarm clock."

They had gone only a few steps toward the door when a *crash* and shattering of glass sounded over their heads.

"What in the world?" Ezra stopped counting. "The lens!" He shot up from the chair and hurried up the stairs.

Nick was only a few steps behind him.

Annie and Clyde stared at each other. A second *thud*, then a third ricocheted down the spiral steps. Annie could stand it no longer. She grabbed up her long skirts and ran to the stairs.

She reached the lantern deck. The beacon blazed, momentarily blinding her. She cried out and threw up her hands. At her feet on the top step a bundle of feathers flopped weakly. Glass shards peppered the floor. Another *thud* and another pelted the glass. "What is it?" She had to shout to be heard above the sound of a hundred wings.

"A bird barrage." Ezra held the door to the catwalk for Nick to squeeze through. "Get below."

"Let me help. What can I do?" A Canada goose flew through the open window and crashed into the center prism of the light. Glass rattled, but nothing broke.

"Get below and help Clyde time the light. We'll worry about the birds."

Annie turned and hurried down the steps, wincing at each impact of a feathered body with glass or metal or brick. Why would geese do this?

Clyde continued to turn, trying to crank with one hand while holding the stopwatch in the other.

She took the watch and held it for him so he could see while he turned. "It's geese. They're flying into the light. One broke a windowpane. Nick went out onto the catwalk. I think he had a broom with him. What would make birds fly into the tower?"

Clyde kept his eyes on the watch. "I've heard of it before. Something goes sideways with them. They act like moths around a candle." Concentration lined his youthful face, his red hair darkening and sticking to his forehead with sweat. "Count for me."

Nick's and Ezra's muffled voices came from overhead. The thudding went on.

Annie took up counting again, huddled on her chair, wondering if the next bird through the window would disable the light completely.

After what seemed like hours—though Annie's watch indicated twenty minutes—the bombardment ceased. Clyde continued to turn the gears and Annie kept on counting, but she strained to hear what was happening upstairs.

At last, feet sounded on the stairs. Ezra came first, his face ashen. Nick followed, shoulders slumped, a smear of blood standing out boldly on his white shirt.

Annie thrust the watch into Ezra's hands and hurried to Nick. "Are you hurt? What happened up there? Is it over?" She touched the red patch, worry over his safety making her hands jerk with small, fluttery movements.

He looked down at her, puzzlement quirking his eyebrows. "I'm fine. The blood isn't mine." His hand covered hers and he brought it down to his side. He didn't let go. Instead he twined their fingers together. With his other hand, he brushed the hair back from her forehead.

A shaken-up feeling jangled through her, like a quarter in a tin can. His handclasp tightened, his palm pressed warmly to hers. She stared into his eyes, wondering what he was thinking, wondering if he knew what affect his presence, his kindness, had on her.

Ezra cleared his throat. "I think you and I, Nick, should stay on watch. Bird barrages are strange things, and quite often they happen in bunches. It wouldn't surprise me if we got another one tonight. Annie, can you handle the timing duties with Clyde?" He held up the silver stopwatch.

Annie nodded. With reluctance, she released Nick's hand. Her shawl had fallen off one shoulder. She groped for it, numbness stealing over her. *Please, God, don't let it happen again. I couldn't stand it. Watch over Nick and Ezra. The catwalk is so small. Don't let them fall.*

"One, two, three. . ."

ten

Nick rubbed his hand across his forehead. Lack of sleep burned his eyes. Only once had he spent a more miserable night, that aboard the freezing, grounded *Bethany* in the teeth of a November gale. This night of battling birds bent on self-destruction, though bad enough, paled in comparison to those nightmare hours.

Stiffness clung stubbornly to his back and shoulders. He rolled his neck. Sleep would be a long way off. They still had to find out why the light was running slow, and they had to clean up the mess. His shoulder ached from the kick of the shotgun. Ezra had brought them each a shotgun from the house when the second attack came. Nick fired so many shells, the barrel of his gun bent from the heat.

Three times the birds came. Several windows in the lantern room were cracked and broken, but the prisms of the lens remained intact. The precious curved glass bore the marks of battle, blood-smeared and smudged, but none had broken. Several dead birds lay on the catwalk and lantern deck. Below, they counted sixteen feathered corpses. Many others had dropped into the lake far below.

Nick doused the beacon and followed Ezra down the stairs into the base of the tower.

Annie sat on the straight-backed chair, her bright hair slipping from its knot. She leaned back, resting her head against the slick, enameled tile on the wall, her face pale, lashes dark against her cheeks. The stopwatch lay in her lap, her fingers curled around it.

Clyde sat along the wall opposite her, arms propped on his upraised knees, wrists limp, hands hanging. He, too, rested his head against the wall, eyes shut. The poor lad had cranked the light for more than five hours straight. He'd probably sleep the clock around.

Ezra went through into the watch room, his shoulders bent. His hair seemed to have whitened overnight, the lines deepening on his face, his eyes growing more sober and haggard as the night wore on.

Soft sunlight crept through the small windows, marching in a spiral around the tower and following the curve of the stairs.

Nick lifted the stopwatch from Annie's relaxed fingers and slipped it into his pocket. He put her arms around his neck and slipped one hand under her knees, the other behind her back. She weighed next to nothing. Her eyelashes fluttered for a moment before falling again, and her head rested against his shoulder. He breathed in the scent of lilacs from her hair.

His heart bumped crazily against his ribs. She felt right in his arms. He recalled how she'd rushed to him, checking to make sure he was all right after his first battle with the birds and how he'd enjoyed her concern, her attention.

That thought brought him up short. What was he thinking? He had no right to court her, to stake a claim. Not only was he unworthy of her after the fiasco with the *Bethany*, but he was also sort of engaged thanks to his grandfather's machination. Unless or until he was released from that engagement, he had no business entertaining thoughts of another woman. Though none of these thoughts kept him from enjoying the feel of her in his arms as he carried her across the grass toward the house.

Imogen met him at the porch door, her face pallid. Her hand shielded the sunlight from her face. She must be in the grips of another headache. "Bring her through here," Imogen whispered and motioned for him to follow her into the parlor.

Nick entered the parlor and knelt to lay Annie on the sofa.

Imogen held a bright crocheted blanket to cover her. He found himself strangely reluctant to let Annie go. He finally withdrew his arms, gently easing her head onto the pillow.

She opened her eyes for a brief instant, her brown gaze looking right into his soul. He blinked, and her eyes closed. A small sigh escaped her. She snuggled into the pillow and slept.

Imogen tucked the blanket around her, edging Nick back. He went into the kitchen, trying to sort out his jumbled feelings.

Imogen met him there. "Poor lass. What a dreadful night for you all. I've got coffee on."

He took a steaming mug from her, blowing across the top to cool the fragrant liquid. "You look done in yourself. Maybe you should lie down for a while, too." The gentle way she eased herself down into a chair, as if her head might come off if she jarred it, caused him concern.

"It's nothing. Just one of my headaches. I took some powders." She rested her cheek on her hand. "Anyway, I got more sleep than anyone on the island last night. The least I can do is keep the coffee hot and get you some breakfast when you're ready."

Nick took a long swallow of coffee, feeling it wash his middle, warming him from the inside out. Though she tried to hide it, he knew her headaches were more than "nothing."

"We won't need breakfast anytime soon, I shouldn't think. Clyde's sleeping like the dead in the tower. Ezra and I have to figure out what's wrong with the light, and we have to reglaze a few windows. We can rustle up some grub when the time comes."

She looked at him shrewdly. "I doubt you've ever cooked for yourself in your life. You have no more notion what goes on in a kitchen than Annie does."

He raised his eyebrows. "What would make you say that?"

"I've been watching you, Nick. You have the best manners

and the most cultivated speech of any assistant lightkeeper I've ever come across. I have a notion you were brought up privileged. You know everything there is to know about the lake and the ships on it, but you're no ordinary deckhand. You have the air of a naval officer about you. You're not hiding something from us that we need to know, are you?"

Nick tried not to squirm under her scrutiny, nor show just how close her evaluation had come to unmasking him. "No, ma'am. I'm not hiding anything from you that you need to know."

Even through the pain in her eyes he could see her brain working. "And I notice how you look at our Annie. You're not planning on breaking her heart, are you? She's a sweet, naive thing, head in the clouds half the time. I won't have you misleading her." Imogen pointed her finger at his chest. "You're a handsome man, Nick Kennedy. Annie's been watching you, too. It wouldn't take much of an effort from you to make her fall in love. Unless your intentions are honorable, I don't think you should trifle with her affections."

Heat curled through Nick's ears and raced up his neck. Not since his grandmother had passed away had he been lectured in such a manner. Imogen reminded him of his grandmother: tiny, energetic, frustrated when her health kept her from living life at a gallop, caring and concerned for those in her charge. "Ma'am, I assure you, I have no intention of dallying with Miss Fairfax. I have other commitments back in Duluth that make a romantic liaison impossible. My fiancée would frown upon such doings." There, that should set Imogen's mind at rest.

Lines formed between her brows. "You're betrothed? I had no idea."

"It's not been publicly announced yet." He was getting in deeper and deeper. "And I'd just as soon keep it quiet around here, too, if you don't mind."

Imogen nodded, though her face bore skepticism.

Nick finished his coffee and headed back to the lighthouse.

❧

"We've been over every inch of the mechanism. I can't find anything wrong. The gears mesh perfectly, the springs are tight, no screws are loose." Nick wiped his hands on a rag and stuffed it into his pocket. "That just leaves one thing."

Ezra and Clyde groaned in unison. "The float."

The lens mechanism "floated" on two hundred fifty ounces of mercury. At a pound per fluid ounce, that meant two hundred fifty pounds of liquid metal to drain and purify.

"Do we have any extra?" Nick eased his tired muscles down until he sat on the floor. He stared out at the lake, listening to the sound of waves gently slapping the rocks at the cliff base that drifted up through the broken windows. Window repair was next on the list of things to do after fixing the light.

"We have one eight-ounce bottle for emergencies." Ezra smoothed his mustache. Earlier he'd put forth the idea that the mercury under the lens had somehow gotten contaminated. It had happened to him once before. Rust flakes had fouled the mercury so the lens wouldn't turn smoothly. They'd kicked around the idea for a while but decided to leave it as a last resort.

Nick turned to Clyde, whose bloodshot eyes bespoke his lack of sleep. "Get two clean buckets and bring a fuel can of kerosene."

"I'll go get the extra mercury should we need it." Ezra started down the stairs after Clyde.

Ezra's hypothesis proved correct. They washed the mercury with kerosene, letting the heavy metal fall through several inches of the oily fuel in the bottom of a bucket. Impurities and rust flakes floated atop the kerosene, easily picked out with a newspaper. The entire operation took about two hours to complete.

When they finished refilling the tank under the lens, Clyde swirled the few drops of mercury left in the bottom of the bucket. "Stuff's amazing." Bright quicksilver beads raced and collided, merged and separated in the bucket.

Nick smiled at how young Clyde looked. The boy had done well. Responsible, polite, conscientious. A good candidate for a ship's officer, given some seasoning.

Nick pulled himself up. How easy it was to slip back into that old frame of mind.

They tested the lamp. With the mercury purified, the beacon rotated with precision.

Nick sighed with relief and clapped Ezra on the back. "Why don't you and Clyde get some shut-eye? The window repair is a one-man job. I can take care of it. Then I'll come in for some food and a nap." He swallowed a yawn. A nap sounded like heaven at the moment.

Glass, glazing points, putty. How thankful Nick was for the supplies. That, at least, he owed to Jasper Dillon. The man kept his lighthouses stocked and ready. Carrying the tools up the stairs, Nick grimaced at how he'd let the little man get under his skin. Henpecked at home. The idea made Nick grin. That explained a lot. Guess he could give the inspector a little leeway.

As he worked, Nick marveled again at the beauty of God's creation. The vista before him couldn't be more spectacular. Aquamarine water, white-tipped waves creaming over, brilliant white-blue sky, snowy clouds, and the north shoreline a faint, dark ribbon in the west. Gulls keened and hovered on the breeze, squawking and bickering.

An ore boat chugged into view. Nick swept up the glasses and held them to his eyes, toying with the focus until the image became clear. The *Kennebrae Cana*, with the *Galilee* in tow.

A lump lodged in his throat. The *Bethany* had been towing the *Galilee* the night the storm hit. Like a fool, he'd cut the *Galilee* loose just outside the harbor to ride out the storm at anchor in the basin. Why hadn't he done the same?

Why had he tried to enter the harbor? The listing and water intake on the *Bethany* hadn't been that bad, had it? The crew might have been able to shift the load and pump out the water if only he'd just dropped anchor like the *Galilee* had. He'd acted in haste and the cost had been high.

His hands ached, and he realized he was gripping the binoculars hard enough to break them. He set the glasses down on the ledge and picked up the putty knife. The glazer's points pricked his fingers, but he welcomed the distraction. Anything to take his mind off his past.

Regular maintenance on the light took him the rest of the morning. He washed every pane and prism. He scrubbed the lantern deck, sweeping up feathers and debris from the repair efforts. Then he trimmed the lamp, setting everything ready for sundown.

He pushed aside thoughts of his old life, of his family, of how things used to be. And he tried without success to ignore the fact that his heart wasn't in the lighthouse. His heart rode the waves racing to catch up with the Kennebrae ships just disappearing over the horizon.

eleven

Life fell into an easy pattern over the next few weeks.

Annie, under Imogen's tutelage, discovered an aptitude for baking, hitherto unknown. She continued to burn, overseason, and otherwise ruin all attempts at stovetop cooking, but she was a marvel with the oven. Her desserts and breads were such a success, the men forgave much in the way of culinary disasters.

Annie managed to secret the Duluth paper out of her bedroom and into the firebox, breathing a sigh of relief as the pages curled and blackened, obliterating news of her escape. She pushed thoughts of her life in Duluth into the back of her mind and concentrated on the here and now, enjoying a freedom she'd never known, blossoming, gaining confidence, deepening her relationships, and finding new facets of her character to explore and strengthen.

Imogen spoke often of spiritual things, teaching Annie through her gentle ways of a deeper, more satisfying relationship with God, one where God wasn't a vengeful or indifferent parent but a loving Father who cared for His children. Annie's faith grew, day by day.

Evenings were her favorite times, especially those evenings when Nick didn't have the early watch. Everyone gathered in the parlor. Imogen would crochet or tat, her rocker creaking softly. Nick would play checkers with Clyde or Ezra. And Annie would read. Though she detested Jasper Dillon, she fell gratefully upon the wooden cupboard of books he'd left, part of the lighthouse library. Each lighthouse on his route received one of the crates of books, to be exchanged at the next inspection.

One night she picked up *King Solomon's Mines*—a choice that would've sent her father into a tirade—and settled herself into a corner of the davenport. Allan Quatermain was such an interesting hero. So stalwart and fearless, and so sad and introspective at times. Annie caressed the cloth cover of the book, her fingers tracing the indentations of vines and leaves, of gold lettering on the spine.

"Since you're starting that book over again, why don't you read it aloud, dear?" Imogen's hook flew in her fingers, poking in and out of the yarn. The ball of wool at her feet tumbled in the basket when she pulled some slack.

Annie cast a glance in the direction of the checkers players. Clyde's bright eyes and grin encouraged her. Nick's darker blue eyes set her breath crowding into the top of her lungs. No matter how she tried to dissuade her heart, she couldn't make herself see sense. He was everything she wanted in a man. It took much discipline on her part to avoid letting her growing feelings for him show.

She opened the book to the dedication and cleared her throat. She had read aloud to Hazel nearly every night while Hazel rocked and knitted or mended. Tears pricked Annie's eyes as she wondered where Hazel was now and if she missed Annie at all. A wave of homesickness rushed over her, receded, then returned to lap about her heart like combers on the beach.

Clyde shifted in his chair, his boots scraping the floor.

The sound brought Annie back, and she began to read.

❧

Nick lost all interest in checkers the moment Annie spoke. Did she know how her voice took on the various characters, each one sounding different?

Clyde, too, ignored the game, wrapped up in the story. Imogen's crochet hook moved slower and slower until it stilled in her hands.

Lamplight raced along Annie's bright curls, her cheeks

flushed slightly. Slender hands held the book, tilting it toward the table lamp next to her.

Nick couldn't help but notice the delicate curve of her neck and the gentle slope of her shoulders. Her shoes stood side by side in front of the sofa, her feet tucked up. He remembered the feel of her in his arms when he carried her in to place her on that very sofa. She had never mentioned it. Neither had he, but he cherished the memory. Even now he imagined he could smell the faint scent of lilacs on her hair.

Nick forced himself to concentrate on the story. He'd look a fool if someone asked him about the plot right now. Annie had a gift, a real gift, for bringing a story to life. In spite of the distractions, he found himself drawn into the tale.

Ezra stomped into the room, breaking the mood.

Nick rose at the expression on Ezra's face.

"There's a ferry off the east side of the island. I could just make it out with the glasses. They're signaling distress. I think they've struck the submerged rocks out there near the bell buoy. We'll have to launch the boat and help them."

Nick nodded. "I'll take Clyde and go. Ezra, you and Annie get down to the dock with blankets. Imogen, get a fire going. There may be injuries." He barely noticed that he'd taken charge of the situation, usurping the authority that rightfully belonged to Ezra. Getting to a wounded vessel quickly meant saving lives.

Clyde sprinted down the dark path through the trees to the dock. Nick followed quickly, picking his way in the lantern light. By the time he reached the dock, Clyde had the canvas tarp off the boat and was loading in the oars.

Nick joined him in the rocking craft. He fastened the lantern to the pole in the stern and sat at the tiller. "Row hard, boy. I'll relieve you when you tire."

Clyde fixed the oars in the oarlocks and bent his back to the task.

Nick leaned on the tiller, curving the boat around the

north end of the island. Once free of the shielding cliff, the bleat of the ship's horn reached them. Above that, faintly, the clang of the bell buoy kept time with the waves.

How had a ferry ended up on the east side of the island? Every lake captain knew of the dangers of the razor-sharp shoals there. All traffic larger than a canoe passed to the west side of Sutton Island.

Fine mist sprayed Nick each time the bow dipped into a trough.

Clyde grunted with effort, but his stroke remained smooth.

"Where'd you learn to row like this?" Nick raised his voice to be heard.

"Father was a lifesaver off the coast of Cape Cod before we moved west." Clyde's teeth gleamed white in the moonlight. "Been rowing since I was a little gupper."

Nick marveled at how God worked, bringing the right people to the right place at the right time. *Please, Lord, let us get to the boat in time.*

From a hundred yards away the ferry's lights flickered on the water. People crowded the deck, shouting. The ship listed hard to port.

Nick caught the tang of smoke in the air from the twin stacks far overhead. He leaned harder on the tiller, and the boat swung around and bumped into the starboard side of the ferry. He read the name *Olivia Star* on the side wheel of the boat.

People rushed forward.

"Hold there!" Nick shouted. "Women and children first. We'll take as many as we can each trip."

Heedless of his words, a wall of humanity surged toward the small craft. One man missed his footing and shot out into the air, landing in the water with a yelp.

When he surfaced, Nick leaned out of the boat and grabbed him by the collar. He dragged the man around the rowboat toward the ferry. "Get up there and wait your turn."

Clyde lifted a child of about six or seven into the boat then reached up for another. "Here you go, lassie. A ride in my nice boat. You sit still, and we'll have you to land in a jiffy." His matter-of-fact voice seemed to calm the children. They huddled together on the seat, eyes wide, but not crying.

"Where's the captain?" Nick scanned the crowd for anyone in authority. "How many passengers are aboard?"

A deckhand in a dirty uniform leaned over the rail. "There's sixteen passengers and eight crew, counting the captain."

"Any injuries?"

"Beyond a few cuts and bruises, I don't think so."

Clyde continued to load passengers until the gunwales dipped toward the water. "This is all we can take this load. We'll be back."

On the return trip, Nick gave the tiller over to a white-faced woman and grasped a pair of oars. Rowing in such a crowd proved difficult, but it hastened their speed.

The water grew choppy when they rounded the west side of the island. "Bail!" Nick's jaw tightened. Waves lapped over the sides of the overloaded boat. "Bail!"

Passengers cupped their hands, throwing the water overboard. One woman removed her hat and used it as a bucket, shoving, pushing, tossing water out.

Relief swamped Nick as the dock came into sight. Annie and Ezra held lanterns high, Ezra out on the end of the dock, Annie on the shore. Nick and Clyde handed passengers up as quickly as they could and started back around the island for another load.

The second return trip was faster, as the passengers were mostly male. The boat could hold fewer of them, but they helped row and bail. On the final trip out to the damaged steamer, nearing exhaustion, Nick and Clyde picked up the last remaining crew members, the first officer, and the captain.

The *Olivia Star* listed farther in the water, her lowest deck now awash. She seemed to have run aground on a single sharp point of rock, tottering and balancing, sliding ever lower as she took on water.

A crew member dumped the captain, a limp tangle of arms and legs in a dark suit, into the bottom of the rowboat. The captain lolled beneath the seats, a livid bruise darkening half his face, a trickle of blood oozing from the corner of his mouth. He mumbled but didn't open his eyes.

"Was he injured in the wreck?" Clyde eased the man's arms aside so he could brace himself at the oars.

The first officer grunted and rolled his eyes. He held his ribs with one arm across his middle, his face ashen. None of the other crewmen said a word.

"You hurt?" Nick steadied the man, placing his hand on the officer's shoulder.

"Ribs."

"Well, rest easy now. We'll have you on shore in no time. Somebody hold this tiller."

Though his arms resembled lake kelp, Nick took up the oars again. Several spots on his fingers and palms burned. He'd have blisters by morning, no doubt.

The rising wind worked against them, blowing against their backs, bucking the small craft.

At last they reached the dock again. Ezra leaned down to pull them up from the boat.

Nick grasped his hand gratefully. "That's all of them. The ship's listing bad, but it's perched on a submerged rock. If it doesn't take on too much water and slide off whatever it's grounded on, it might be salvageable." *Like the* Bethany. Nick leaned against the dock piling, wrapping the bowline of the rowboat securely. The thought jabbed him like a poke in the eye.

Annie stood at the far end of the dock. Why didn't she come out?

He beckoned to her, but she shook her head, her face

ghostly in the light of the lantern she held up to guide the refugees toward the path. He staggered toward her, body screaming from the rescue efforts.

When he got close, she bit her lip, tears wetting her cheeks. "You're all right? You got everyone?"

"We got everyone." He gave in to the urge and put his arm around her shoulders, hugging her into his side. "Nice to know someone was here worrying about us."

She stayed in his embrace a moment then seemed to collect herself.

He dropped his arm from around her and stepped back, wondering if he had offended her with his familiarity.

"I'm glad you're all right. I prayed for you as hard as I could." She brushed her skirts and ducked her head. "We'd best get up the hill and help Imogen. I don't know where we're going to put all these people."

He took the lantern and offered her his arm for the hike up the hill.

❧

The smell of damp wool and coffee hit Annie in the face when she walked into the kitchen. Woebegone looks greeted her. People huddled near the stove, and Imogen filled cups. A kettle whistled.

"I'll take that." Annie lifted the coffeepot from Imogen's hands. She bent her head to whisper in Imogen's ear, "What are we going to do? Where can we put so many people?"

"We'll manage, dear. They'll have to sleep on the floor, that's all. It's how we're going to feed them that has me praying." Imogen patted Annie's hand. "God will figure things out. He hasn't failed us yet."

Annie shook her head, smiling. God *was* going to have to figure things out, because Annie was fresh out of ideas. If she fed them any of her own cooking, they'd likely take to the lake and try to swim to shore just to escape.

Imogen tore up a bed sheet and Annie helped her wrap

the ribs of the first officer. That man, clammy and gray, they put on the sofa, propped up with plenty of pillows. He thanked them over and over in a shallow, breathy voice. Imogen dosed him with tea and a bit of laudanum from the medical kit, and he drifted off to sleep moments later.

The captain proved a more difficult patient. He mumbled and thrashed, face screwed up in a thundercloud grimace. Annie tried to hold a cold compress to his bruised head, but he kept swatting her away. He reeked of a most foul odor, one Annie couldn't place. Obviously the smack on the head had disoriented the man to the point of delirium. He finally subsided in Imogen's rocker, so Annie left him there, snoring like a fog signal.

Clyde and Nick got most of the men bedded down in the assistant keepers' quarters. Three had to settle for pallets on the parlor floor in the main house. Annie gave up her room to a mother and her two small daughters and moved in with Imogen. Nick, Clyde, and Ezra would take turns sleeping on a cot in the fog-house.

By the time everyone was settled for the night, the clock struck two. Annie dragged herself up the stairs. Her hair had long since given up staying in its knot. She flipped it back over her shoulder with a tired hand. Breakfast for thirty? It didn't bear thinking about.

She shrugged into her nightgown, keeping the lamp low in deference to Imogen, who was already asleep. Annie slipped between the sheets, not bothering to braid her hair for the night. She'd battle the snarls in the morning. If she wasn't so tired, she'd take the time to examine just how relieved she was to see Nick come back safe and sound. . .that and how wonderful his embrace had been.

twelve

God proved Himself trustworthy again the next morning. One of the women rescued from the ferry was the ship's cook. She took over the kitchen, fixing breakfast for thirty without displaying any of the panic Annie would've felt. Annie turned the entire operation over to the five women from the ship and concentrated on caring for Imogen, who once more found herself victim of a sick headache.

The children, the most resilient of the group, bounced outside to explore the moment they were excused from the table. Annie took one look at the overloaded dishpan and blew out a breath, fanning wisps of hair off her forehead. She needn't have worried. The women were more than willing to pitch in and help. Annie left them to it and went into the parlor to check on the two wounded men.

How Hazel would laugh to see Annie now, changing bed linens, administering medicine, acting the hostess for two dozen unexpected guests. Annie, who had never cooked, cleaned, or cared for her own clothing. Hazel would hardly know her. Annie hardly knew herself.

She opened the drapes a crack, saw that the man on the sofa was awake, and pulled them a bit wider. Sunlight streamed in, tracking across the polished maple floor, picking out motes in the air. "How are you feeling?" She pulled the blanket higher around the injured man.

He tried to speak, but only a croak came out.

Annie helped him sit a little straighter and held a glass of water to his cracked lips.

"My name is Saunders. Jared Saunders." He hugged his ribs, his lips tight. "Thank you for all you are doing. Are the passengers all right?"

Annie nodded, twisting her hands in her apron. "They're fine. Everyone's breakfasted but you two." She gestured to the captain, sagging in the rocker, face slack. "Would you like me to bring you some food?"

He shook his head, throwing a look of disgust toward the captain. "No, I couldn't eat a thing. Perhaps some coffee?"

"Coffee it is. What about the captain? Should I wake him?"

"I wouldn't advise it." Saunders's voice held a dry irony.

The captain must not be a morning person. She'd let him sleep. After the trauma last night, sleep was probably the best thing for him.

She whirled to go back to the kitchen, colliding with Nick in the doorway. His hands came up and cupped her shoulders, turning her insides to water. She hadn't seen him since last night. He'd had the early watch in the tower. Shadows clouded his blue eyes. No wonder, with the rescue and then having to stand watch.

"Nick, good morning." Did that sound as breathless as she felt?

"Good morning, Annie. How are your patients?" He backed up a step and dropped his hands to his sides. A faint bristle of whiskers covered his unshaven cheeks, and tired lines spidered out from the corners of his eyes.

"Mr. Saunders asked for a cup of coffee. I haven't checked on the captain yet. He seems to be sleeping quite soundly."

Nick bent over the captain, scrutinizing the bruise on the man's temple. He sniffed, frowned, and then poked the man in the shoulder. "Quite soundly." Nick's voice held a strange tightness.

"Come into the kitchen and I'll get you breakfast." She laughed. "Don't worry, it wasn't cooked by me. It will be quite edible, I assure you." She turned to Saunders. "I'll be right back with your coffee."

૨.

Nick followed Annie into the kitchen. Women washed and wiped plates, carrying them into the pantry, bustling back out, chattering. He'd come through the front door of the house, hoping to catch Ezra alone in his office and avoid talking to anyone else until he spoke with his boss.

"There he is." One of the women, tall, with wiry red hair, rushed over to him and wrung his hand. "We want to thank you for saving us last night. I don't know what would've become of us if you hadn't come along." The women crowded around him, professing their gratitude, some wiping tears. One even kissed his cheek.

Annie caught his eye, obviously enjoying his embarrassment. She filled a coffee cup and went back into the parlor.

All the while, anger simmered in his gut. Last night had been too fraught with danger and exertion to be sure, but one look at the captain this morning had confirmed Nick's suspicions. He had to talk to Ezra.

The tall redhead pushed him down into a chair and plunked a bowl of steaming oatmeal in front of him. "Now, you eat up, Mr. Kennedy. There's plenty more where that came from."

Nick reached for a biscuit in the basket on the table, broke it open, and spread it with jam. He bit into it. It was good, but nothing like his Annie's biscuits. He stopped chewing. *His* Annie?

As if his thoughts conjured her up, she came back into the kitchen. He rose. "Have you seen Ezra?"

"Sit down, please. He and Clyde went to the east side of the island to look at the ferry awhile ago. He said they'd be back shortly."

Nick nodded. He finished the biscuit, ate a few bites of the oatmeal to be polite, and then stood. Before he could wend his way through the women, Ezra opened the back porch door and stepped in.

"The ferry survived, still perched on that rock. She's about a hundred yards east of the bell buoy. Looks like she might've run smack over it, the way it's bent. Someone will need to get out there and repair that buoy before too long."

"Can you come into the parlor?" Nick jerked his head toward the door.

Annie took up the coffeepot and headed into the parlor just ahead of them. She filled Saunder's cup again then picked up the bottle of laudanum from the end table.

Nick waited until she'd given the man a dose. "Annie, if you don't mind, I need to speak to—"

Nick's words were cut off by a growl from the captain. He stirred in his chair like a bear waking from hibernation, gripped his temples between his meaty paws, and groaned. "It hurts."

Annie darted to his side and knelt down. "Don't try to move, sir. You've had quite a knock on the head. I'll get you a headache powder right away."

Nick took hold of Annie's arm and lifted her out of the way. "Don't bring him anything." His voice was sharper than he'd intended.

Her eyes widened, and she looked down at his grip on her elbow.

His hand fell away. "I'm sorry. I need to speak to the captain before you give him any medicine."

Saunders propped himself up on his elbows. "His name is—"

"I don't care what his name is. To me, he's just another bottom feeder." Nick hauled the captain up by his lapels. He sniffed. Alcoholic fumes emanated from the man to the point Nick thought the captain might burst into flames if he got too near a candle. "You're drunk."

"Leave me alone." The captain's words slurred. His eyes looked terrible, bloodshot, with pinprick pupils.

"Were you manning the pilothouse when the ship went

aground?" Nick glared at the sodden excuse for a lake captain. When the man didn't answer, Nick turned to the injured officer on the sofa.

Saunders lay back, eyes closed to mere slits. He nodded. "Captain had the wheel. Threw us all out of the pilothouse just after sundown. I went below to talk to the crew. The captain had been drinking off and on all day."

"And you let him take the wheel?"

Saunders gave a low chuckle then groaned and held his ribs, panting in shallow puffs. His face twisted in a wry grimace, half pain, half shame. "He used considerable force. He's a brute when he's drinking. I didn't get these bad ribs in the wreck. He tossed me out of the pilothouse like a piece of driftwood. I hit against the rail. Lucky I didn't go over into the water. I made it down to the engine room, barely. We were discussing a mutiny when the ferry ran aground."

The captain wavered on unsteady legs. "A mutiny? I'll have your liver, you two-faced coyote." He clutched his head again, his complexion turning gray-green. "Where's my whiskey?"

"How dare you!" Nick's jaw ached, his teeth clamped hard. He shook the man.

The captain howled. "My head."

Ezra stepped forward and placed his hand on Nick's forearm. "Maybe we should sober him up before—"

Nick shrugged Ezra off, too angry to think. "He wounded his own crewman on purpose. He's soaked with liquor. This is dereliction of duty in all its worst forms, putting women and children at risk for no reason other than unbridled lust for liquor." A nasty taste grew in Nick's mouth. He turned back to the pathetic officer. "You were so drunk you ran over a bell buoy and grounded your ship at the foot of a lighthouse. You endangered the lives of your passengers and crew. You don't deserve to be a lake captain."

The drunkard's chin came up, a look of belligerent contempt

gleaming from his bloodshot eyes. "Hah. You're one to talk. I know who you are, Kenne—"

Nick's fist shot out and caught the captain in the jaw.

The man's head snapped back, his eyes rolled, and he sagged in Nick's grasp.

Pain shot up Nick's arm, but he disregarded it.

Annie gasped.

Nick saw her out of the corner of his eye.

She put her hand over her mouth, her brown eyes wide in shock.

He gulped for air, tense as an anchor chain in a storm.

Annie blinked, staring at him as if at a stranger.

The anger drained from him. He released the man's lapels.

The captain sagged to the floor, sniffling and moaning.

Nick held up his hand to Annie, wanting to apologize, but the words lodged in his throat. He wasn't sorry for the punch. He'd gag if he tried to say he was. But he was sorry to have been such a brute in her presence. He swung away from her shocked face, shoulders quivering, fists clenched.

Ezra's troubled eyes met Nick's. "I wish you hadn't done that, son."

Before Nick could respond, the captain pushed himself to his knees. Spittle and blood flew when he opened his mouth. Though slurred, Nick understood him perfectly. "You'll be sorry for this. I'm Grover Dillon. My brother Jasper is your boss. He'll have your job for this." A thick sausagelike finger poked the air.

Annie's gasp sliced through Nick's heart. A ton weight pushed against his chest. He had to get away before he took another swing at that pathetic man. The doorframe wavered. He blinked, clearing his vision, then turned on his heel and strode out through the kitchen into the sunshine.

Emotions bounced around inside him like ball bearings dropped on a concrete floor. He turned his face to the warm rays, taking deep breaths, trying to calm himself. What had possessed him to punch that man? Violence hadn't solved anything. It only made his situation worse. Nick's hand throbbed in time with his heart.

What hurt the most was knowing that not all of his anger had been righteous. Had he punched the man for being a drunkard or had he punched him to keep him from revealing Nick's identity? Nick knew the truth, though admitting it shamed him to the core.

He hung his head. *Lord, I'm a fool. I acted without thinking. Forgive me, please. And help me to bear it if the captain broadcasts the truth.*

The thought of the hurt in Annie's eyes should the truth come out made Nick wince. He had to avoid that at all costs. Nick flexed his hand and lifted his chin. At least his day couldn't get any worse. He nodded to two of the ferry refugees on the cobbled path.

"Say"—one of the men stopped on his way into the house and turned to study Nick's face—"you look awfully familiar. Haven't I seen you in Duluth?"

thirteen

When Nick volunteered to handle extra watches in the tower, Ezra couldn't hide his relief. A man of peace, Ezra no doubt wanted to keep Nick from punching anyone else.

In the two days since putting his fist into the drunk's face, Nick had remained in the tower and watch room. Clyde or Ezra brought him his meals, making him feel like a prisoner. Of Annie he'd seen nothing. His gut churned each time he thought of her. What might she say if the truth came out?

Would Dillon keep his mouth shut? Perhaps Nick should come clean with Ezra at least. For two days he waited for his secret to come home to roost, but nothing happened. His only escape from the lighthouse came when he and Clyde took one of the ferry's crew over to the grounded ship to offload some of their supplies to help feed and house the passengers.

Nick now stood on the catwalk outside the lantern deck, a fresh breeze ruffling his hair and making his pant legs flap like flags. He swept the horizon with the field glasses.

A tiny blot to the north gradually became more defined. A stack emerged, white steam trailing back. Gleaming decks and a red side wheel plowing the water. He waited. The boat came close enough for him to read the name, though he knew it by heart. *Jenny Klamath* in black and gold letters.

A gull rose above the level of the cliff and hung in the air only a dozen feet from the tower.

"We'll get these passengers loaded, especially *Captain* Grover Dillon"—contempt dripped from Nick's words—"and anyone else who might recognize me. Then things can return to normal."

The gull cocked his head, pinfeathers fluttering. He keened as if in answer then plummeted toward the water.

Several hours before, Ezra had raised the flag on the pole at the end of the dock, signaling for the ferry to stop on its way down-lake. The *Jenny Klamath* would be on the watch for it, as they always were when passing the light, and would soon slow and head toward the dock. The ferry's shallow draw allowed it to pull right up to the dock, unlike the supply ships which had to anchor well offshore and use a launch.

Would Annie be at the dock? Maybe he should go down there. No, better not to risk Dillon or one of the other passengers blowing the whistle.

A blast of the ferry's horn indicated she'd seen the flag. Nick kept the glasses on her until she disappeared behind the trees on the west side of the island.

The screen door on the house slapped repeatedly as refugees ventured out and headed across the clearing toward the gap in the trees that marked the path down to the dock.

Footsteps clanged on the metal staircase, and the heavy iron door scraped open behind Nick. He turned.

Clyde's blazing mop poked through the small opening. His blue eyes squinted in the sunshine. "Thought you'd be up here. Guess you'll be gladder than anyone to have all these people gone." His white shirt fluttered and flapped, molding to his narrow chest and wiry arms. "Captain Dillon is still growling like a bear with a bee-stung behind."

Nick lifted the glasses to his eyes once again. "Did he say anything more about me?"

"No, and that's mighty odd, because he's complained about everything else. Whenever your name comes up, he gets a weird gleam in his eye. I'd watch out if I were you. He means you no good, and that's the truth."

Clyde's open, sunny personality both refreshed and chided Nick. So many weeks of hiding his own identity, of watching every word, grated on him. The more he grew to like and admire Ezra, Imogen, and Clyde—and Annie, particularly Annie—the more distasteful his duplicity grew.

Clyde leaned his hip against the rail and crossed his arms, seemingly oblivious to the one-hundred-plus-foot drop to the water below. "Nick, have you ever courted a girl?"

The glasses came down. "What?"

Clyde's cheeks reddened until his freckles disappeared. He shrugged, whipped out his handkerchief, and rubbed a spot on one of the windowpanes. "A girl. Have you ever courted one?"

"I can't say that I have."

Clyde sighed. "Well, it's about time you did."

"Excuse me?"

"Miss Annie. I think you should court her. I was going to give it a try myself, her being so pretty and nice and all, but she'd never go for a guy like me. Anyone who's been around you both for more than ten minutes can see she's got feelings for you."

Warmth blossomed in Nick's chest. She did? In spite of himself he had to ask, "How do you know?"

"The last two days while you've been hiding in the tower"—he gave Nick a knowing look—"she's been wandering around like a lost kitten. No smiles, no laughter, and every time one of us comes back from bringing a meal to you, she asks how you are."

Nick pondered Clyde's words. Was it true? Could she have feelings for him? "If she cares so much, why didn't she come over and see me for herself?"

Clyde's boots scraped on the metal grating. "I don't know. Maybe she thought you didn't want her to. Or maybe she didn't want to look like she was setting her cap for you, especially since you haven't let her know you'd like to court her. Girls are funny that way." His lips pursed and he nodded, all the wisdom of his twenty years gleaming in his eyes.

"And how is it you know so much about women?"

"I have nine sisters. A fellow has to learn a few things just to survive in a house like that."

Nick handed him the field glasses. "You can take the watch. I'm going to get cleaned up."

He mulled over Clyde's words. Did he want them to be true? And if so, what was he prepared to do about them?

❧

Annie took the last glass from Imogen and placed it on the pantry shelf. She squared up the bottles and tins of spices, each label facing frontward, each container even with the ones next to it. "We'll have to make note of the extra supplies we used for the guests."

"You've made marvelous progress, Annie." Imogen spread the damp tea towel on the bar on the inside of the pantry door. "Inspector Dillon won't find anything to cavil at when he returns."

Annie laughed, grimacing. "After the first disastrous inspection, I had nowhere to go but up. And I owe it all to you. You've been so patient. And the men. They've borne my ruined attempts at cooking with great fortitude. I think Nick wondered if he might starve to death when he caught sight of my first attempt at cooking oatmeal."

Imogen preceded Annie into the kitchen and poured them each a cup of coffee. "It's a good thing you've become such a marvelous baker. Cookies and pies and apple dumplings cover a multitude of sins." She smiled, her dark eyes glowing with friendship.

Annie took the cup Imogen offered and sat at the table. The silence wrapped around her like supple silk. No more crowds, no more people asking her for things, no more surly captain holding his head and swearing at her. Now things could return to the tranquil pattern of before. And Nick could come down from the tower once more.

Nick. She could admit to herself how much she'd missed

him over the past few days, missed his easy banter with Clyde, missed reading aloud with him in the room, missed their discussions of novels and politics and nature when the reading was done. And most of all she had missed him during yesterday morning's worship service. Though the parlor had been crowded with people, for Annie it had seemed empty without Nick to lead them in prayer, to discuss the passage read.

Imogen sat down opposite Annie, a worried frown on her brow. "Annie, I know it isn't any of my business, but I've noticed how you watch Nick and how your face lights up when he comes into the house."

Annie focused her gaze on Imogen, heat easing into her neck and up her cheeks.

Imogen moved her cup in small circles, staring into it. "Nick is a fine man, to be sure, but you need to be careful. Living here in such close quarters, sometimes you can feel things for someone, or think someone feels things for you, when it's really just a matter of proximity." She looked up, dark eyes entreating Annie to understand. "I just ask you to take care. You're young, and Nick's very handsome. But we all have lives away from here: other things, family, commitments, and such. Just go slow, all right?"

Annie dropped her gaze to her lap and twined her fingers together. Was it just proximity? Would she feel the same about Nick if she'd met him on a busy street in Duluth? "I appreciate the warning, Imogen. I really do. You don't have to worry. I won't rush into anything. I'd best get back to work, and you should rest. You've worked too hard the past few days. I'll straighten up the parlor myself."

She was still folding blankets and moving chairs when Nick came into the house. She knew his footsteps instantly, and her heart thumped more quickly in response. In spite of her words to Imogen about not rushing, she couldn't help her response to him.

"Annie." He stood in the doorway, his hair windblown. Caution clouded his eyes, a wariness she hadn't seen in him before.

"Nick." She dropped the afghan onto the back of the rocker, so happy to see him after his self-imposed isolation. "There's fresh coffee." She joined him in the kitchen, lifting down an enamel mug.

"Annie, I want to apologize for my behavior." He sounded as if he had a ball of yarn in his throat.

She handed him the coffee, puzzled.

"I shouldn't have been such a brute in your presence." His blue eyes studied her, making her skin tingle. "That captain deserved a thrashing, but I should've taken things outside. I'm sorry. No lady should have to watch such undignified behavior."

"Please don't apologize. The captain got nowhere near what he deserved. I'm only sorry it drove you out of the house for a few days."

He took her hand, sending ribbons of heat swirling through her. "You're most generous. I'd like to make it up to you somehow. I'll tell you what. I have to fix the bell buoy on the east side of the island and check on the ship. Salvagers showed up this morning to start patching her and getting her off the rocks. Why don't you come with me on the lake? It's a warm day. We might even do a little fishing."

Annie's mouth went dry. Go out on the lake in that tiny boat? Cold sweat prickled her skin like hundreds of ants. With everything in her heart she wanted to go with him, to spend time alone with him. But fear cloaked her. Memories mocked her.

"Annie?" He stepped closer, his clasp on her hand tightening.

"I'd like to, Nick, but—"

"I know you don't like the water much." He stood close. "I've seen how you won't venture out on the dock. Falling into the lake your first day here must've been terribly frightening. But that's in the past, and you're fine now. I wouldn't let anything happen to you. I'd really like you to come."

No. I can't. Never. I'd die of fright.

"Yes, Nick. I'd love to go."

fourteen

Walking down the trail through the trees to the dock, Annie wondered for the thousandth time in the past hour what had possessed her to agree to this. Her other hand rested in the crook of Nick's elbow, the muscles playing beneath his shirtsleeve doing nothing to calm her jumping heart.

Lord, what was I thinking? I can't do this. I can't. How can I cry off without looking a fool? Help me. Help me get through this. I can't do this.

Her mind kept up a constant prayer. She cast a glance back up the slope through the trees to the tower. The beginning of the Proverb Ezra had read at services her first Sunday on the island played through her head.

"The name of the Lord is a strong tower: the righteous runneth into it, and is safe."

A strong tower. God is a strong tower. A refuge.

A trickle of calm flowed into the maelstrom inside her. They reached the foot of the dock. She could do this. With God's help, she could do this.

"I can't do this." She stopped the instant her feet scraped on the damp wood. Her hand slipped out of Nick's arm and she scooted back to the safety of dry land. "I can't."

He turned quizzical eyes upon her. "The dock's sturdy. Look." He jumped and landed on the boards with a *thud*. "Solid as the cliff she's fastened to." He smiled, his teeth white against his tanned skin. "Well, maybe not that solid, but no woman as small as you is going to unsettle it." He held out his hand, beckoning her to follow. "I'll keep you from falling in again."

A strong tower. A strong tower. A strong tower.

Against everything within her, her hand reached out for his. Here in the lea of the island, the breeze sighed and the waves swished and gurgled almost playfully. She looked down but quickly raised her eyes. She didn't want to see the water moving between the boards under the dock. It might sound playful, but she knew the dangers lurking there.

She suddenly recalled his last words. "I didn't fall off. I was pushed." Her chin came up. The very idea that she'd fall off the dock like some ninnyhammer.

He shook his head. "Naw, I think you weren't looking where you were going and tumbled in."

"I did not. Clyde hit me with a mailbag. You were there. You saw the whole—" She stopped when he laughed.

"Look, you made it all the way to the boat." Nick nodded toward the small craft bobbing on the waves. He wore a smug expression.

"You teased me on purpose." The knot in her stomach loosened a coil.

"Worked, didn't it?" He stepped into the boat and braced his feet against the rocking motion. "I'll help you in. And this time, no throwing up on my boots. It's calm as a baby's naptime out there today. You shouldn't get seasick." His eyes twinkled. He beckoned for her to come closer to the edge.

What on earth was she doing getting into a rowboat? Her feelings for Nick had addled her brains.

He put his hands on her waist. Her fingers shook as she settled them on his broad shoulders. As if she weighed nothing, he lifted her, swinging her into the boat. She sagged onto a seat, her heart knocking wildly as the boat wobbled.

Tools lay in the bottom of the rowboat, clanking gently. Nick slipped the rope from its mooring and used an oar to shove away from the dock.

Annie put her hand on her chest, trying to assist her breathing. How was it all the wide outdoors didn't have enough air to fill her lungs? Her knuckles turned white and ached from her one-handed grip on the gunwale.

Nick fitted the oars into the oarlocks and pulled. The boat shot away from the dock.

A strong tower, a strong tower, astrongtowerastrongtower. "A strong tower."

"What's that?"

She opened her eyes, barely realizing she'd closed them. Nick eyed her questioningly.

"I was quoting that Bible verse we read the first Sunday I was here. Proverbs 18:10. 'The name of the Lord is a strong tower: the righteous runneth into it, and is safe.' I've read that verse over and over, and I learn something new each day about how God is a strong tower."

Water rushed against the hull, slapping, chuckling, taunting her. She stared at Nick's face, trying to draw strength from him, trying not to let the memories clawing inside her head overtake her.

Nick looked over his shoulder and up the cliff face to where the lighthouse emerged as they rounded the north end of the island. "That's a good verse for here."

A shout reached them from overhead. Clyde leaned over the rail, waving down to them.

"He's a nice boy." Annie pried her hand from the edge of the seat and dared a quick wave up to him.

Nick laughed. "He's older than you are."

"Is he? He seems so young."

"Tell me about yourself, Annie. I know nothing about you except you love to read and you make a terrific apple pie. Oh, and to steer clear of your oatmeal." He eyed her with a grin, waiting for her response.

She made a face at his teasing. What could she say? *My name is really Anastasia, and I've run away from home? I'm the daughter of a mining tycoon who wants me to marry a complete stranger in order to bolster his fortune?*

She settled for the story she'd told Imogen. It was true,

if not complete. "I grew up in Duluth. My father works in mining, in Hibbing mostly. My mother passed away when I was young."

"Any brothers or sisters?"

A hard lump formed in Annie's throat. "One brother, but he died when I was small. What about you? Any siblings?"

"Two brothers." He shrugged. "One older and one a few minutes younger. I'm a twin."

"Really? Does he look like you?" She shook her head at the thought. There couldn't be another man as handsome as Nick Kennedy.

"Similar, but not identical. He's back East right now learning a trade."

"What about your parents?" She relished this chance to get to know him better.

"My mother died in childbirth. My father followed not long after in a carriage crash. My brothers and I were raised by my grandparents."

"Have you always been in the lighthouse service?"

He shook his head, looking past her shoulder. "No, but I've always worked around or on the lake." The chop increased, the breeze tugging at his hair. He pulled on the oars, eyes staring far away, watching the water, the cliffs, the sky. He had no fear, completely at ease. "A great day for making good time on the lake. The *Jenny Klamath* should be almost to Duluth by now."

She nodded, not taking her eyes from his face. If only this boat wasn't so wide she could grip both sides. Her muscles ached with tension.

Gulls squabbled overhead, diving and hovering, white-gray flashes in the afternoon sunshine. A loon bobbed on the waves near the cliff base. It dived, disappearing from view only to pop up a dozen yards away, lightning fast.

"There are some mighty big fish that live amongst these rocks. Sturgeon the size of lifeboats."

She questioned him with a glance. "Lifeboats?" She didn't want to think about lifeboats, nor the need for them.

"Well, maybe not that big. But there are some monsters down there just waiting to be caught."

Monsters. "Do you think Captain Dillon will cause trouble? I've never seen a man so angry."

Nick shrugged. "He might, but it would be risky for him. The passengers and crew can testify that he was stone drunk the night of the wreck. He'll lose his job if nothing else, and he might even face criminal charges. Getting revenge on me might be the least of his worries."

"Was he telling the truth about being the inspector's brother?"

Nick grinned. "Who would claim to be Jasper Dillon's brother if he really wasn't?"

Annie surprised herself by laughing. "True. Though I didn't see any family resemblance, unless you count overall crankiness."

They swung around the north side of the island and headed east. The chop increased, small creaming froth appearing on the tops of some of the waves.

"You all right? No seasickness?" He pulled his feet away from her. "My boots aren't in danger, are they?"

Annie shook her head, smiling in spite of the fear. This wasn't so bad. *A strong tower. A strong tower.*

Nick steered them away from the island, covering an expanse of open water.

Annie caught her first glimpse of the stranded ferry. Several boats dotted the surface around the ship, men striding the decks, throwing ropes to one another, hammering and pounding.

"They've started the repairs. I don't think it will take them long. She isn't really wounded as much as just stuck. If they can get her off the rocks without inflicting too much damage, they can tow her in. I see they've brought bilge pumps.

Maybe they can pump fast enough to compensate for the water she might take on between here and Two Harbors. If she isn't too badly crippled, they might even tow her to Duluth where they can more easily make the repairs." Nick swung their boat around to get a better look at the lakeward side of the ferry. "Good thing she's shallow drafted. An oar boat would've ripped wide open on these rocks." His voice sounded far away and sad, as if recalling events that brought him pain. He shook his head and pulled on the oars again.

From a distance a faint clanking reached Annie's ears. The bell buoy. She prayed it wouldn't take Nick long to make the repairs, though she had to admit, being out here in a boat wasn't as bad as she'd feared.

They approached the buoy. Nick whistled. "He hit her square. All she needs is a little hammering to straighten her out. That and a new coat of paint, but we'll have to wait on that until we get some on the next tender." Nick shipped his oars, allowing the boat to glide alongside the red and white frame of the buoy. He reached out and grabbed the buoy, halting their forward progress. "Hand me that line, would you, please?"

Annie glanced down to the pile of rope at her feet. She groped for the end with one hand, frustration clenching her stomach when she couldn't unwind it properly. She'd have to let go and use both hands. Finger by finger she peeled away from the gunwale. Her heart thudded in her ears. She almost laughed when she realized she was pushing down with her legs, trying to anchor herself more firmly in the boat. The line untwisted, and she handed it to Nick. A rickety breath rushed into her lungs. This wasn't so bad, was it?

Then Nick stood up. The boat bucked side to side, a little water slipping in over the edge.

Annie pitched toward the lake, a shriek erupting from her throat. At the last instant her hands locked onto the seat.

Nick looked at her over his shoulder, tying the boat to

the buoy. "What?" He scanned the water around them. He studied her as he bent to pick up a hammer, sending the boat rocking again.

"Don't! Please!" To her shame, sobs bolted out of her throat. She sank to the floor of the boat, still gripping the seat, eyes clamped shut. The sound of water roared in her ears. She imagined it closing over her head, shutting out the world of light and air, imprisoning her within its frigid clasp.

"What's all this?" Nick's warm hands closed over her shoulders.

She clutched at him, eyes popping open, lungs gulping air in great gasps.

He knelt in the bottom of the boat, enfolded her in his arms, and stroked her hair. "Annie? What happened? You were doing so well."

She gripped his shirtfront. "Don't stand up. Don't. You'll tip us over. Please, don't stand up."

"I won't." He held her tight against his chest, letting her cry. "Shh, it's all right. You're safe, Annie. I won't tip the boat over. I promise."

The bell clanked over and over with the rocking of the boat.

She sniffed and hiccupped.

He gallantly pushed a handkerchief into her icy hands.

She gripped it in her fist as she clung to his shirtfront. "I'm sorry. I thought I could do this. I'm so sorry. Please, take me back."

"I'm the one who should apologize. I pushed you too hard. We'll go back now." He settled her on the seat and picked up his oars. With mighty pulls they surged over the surface of the water.

Annie couldn't bear to look at Nick. She had failed. He must think she was an idiot. She *was* an idiot. One little lurch of the boat and she turned into a quivering mass of hysteria. She bent her head and kept her eyes on her shoe tips until the boat bumped into the dock.

Nick began to tie the craft off.

Annie didn't wait for him to help her. She scrambled onto the planks and all but ran to dry land.

Hard thuds followed her, and Nick's hand gripped her elbow. "Annie, wait."

Tears of humiliation and guilt ran down her cheeks. "Let me go, please, Nick."

"I can't let you go like this. Tell me what happened out there."

"No, I can't." She struggled in his grasp, but his grip tightened.

He gave her a little shake. "Annie, tell me."

The truth burst out, though it cost her mightily to voice the words. "My brother died on that lake. And I killed him."

His hands fell away from her, and she made her escape, sobs nearly strangling her as she struggled up the steep slope, away from his look of shocked horror.

❦

Nick stood still for one moment then headed after her. He castigated himself for being so prideful, thinking if he just got her out in a boat she'd be fine, that *he* could cure her of her fear. When was he going to learn not to be so arrogant?

He heard her before he saw her. Her dry, rasping sobs pierced his heart. She reached the clearing, panting, shoulders shaking.

"Annie, stop."

She halted, arms stiff at her sides, one hand clutching his handkerchief. Her chin nearly touched her chest. A tear dropped to the ground.

He couldn't help it. She looked so forlorn and helpless. He put his arms around her, tucking her head under his chin. She smelled of flowers and sunshine, and he didn't care that someone might see them. He only wanted to take away her hurt or share it somehow.

"I'm sorry, Annie. I had no idea." He brushed a kiss across her hair. "Please tell me what happened. I don't believe for one minute you killed your brother."

Contentment settled into his chest when she put her arms around his waist. They stood like that for a long moment, too short a time in his mind, before she pulled back, wiping her eyes with his handkerchief.

He led her to a fallen log on the edge of the clearing, crouching on one knee before her and keeping hold of her hands. "Tell me, please."

"It happened a long time ago, when I was six. Neville was eight. We were visiting friends of my parents who had a house on the lake. There were no other children to play with and nothing to do, so Neville and I ventured down to the shore to throw rocks into the water." She twisted her fingers together in his grasp, not looking at him.

"Go on."

Her delicate throat worked as she swallowed and continued. "Father told us to stay off the dock, but we were bored. Neville bet me I couldn't run to the end of the dock, touch the boat shed, and run back faster than he could." A wisp of a smile tugged the corner of her mouth. "He was always betting me one thing or another, and I was always trying to prove I was as good as he was. Father never had much time for me, but he doted on Neville. Took him everywhere, treated him like a pet. I guess I always wanted to be as good as Neville so my father would love me, too." She hiccupped.

"We raced a couple times. Each time Neville won. I couldn't bear his taunting, so I challenged him to get into the rowboat tied to the dock. Neither of us could swim, and this was the height of daring, especially considering how furious Father would be if he caught us." Her voice caught for a moment. Nick released one of her hands to brush several strands of hair off her cheek and tuck them behind her ear.

He cupped her cheek and stared into her troubled brown eyes, trying to give her strength.

"Neville said just getting into the boat would be too easy. He bet me I'd never have the nerve to get in the boat with him and row out a ways. He told me no girl would ever be that brave."

She hung her head, but he put his finger under her chin and raised her face to the light. When he opened his mouth to tell her she didn't have to go on, she shook her head and rushed on as if now that she'd begun she had to finish the story. "We got in the boat, and Neville untied it. He pushed us away from the dock. I couldn't believe he'd actually done it. The oars were so big, Neville couldn't manage them both. He ended up pulling on only one, and we twisted and turned circles, all the while drifting farther and farther away from the dock. I got more and more scared, and I started to cry. I begged Neville to get us to shore. He shouted at me to quit crying and grab the other oar. I tried to, but I knocked it into the water and it floated too far away for me to reach."

Her tears flowed freely. Sorrowful memories filled her eyes. She didn't see Nick at all, it seemed, so focused on the past, only long-ago images filled her mind. "Neville yelled at me, calling me stupid. I suppose if we'd both kept our heads, someone would've rescued us, but we panicked. Neville stood up in the boat to try to reach out with his paddle to get back the oar I'd dropped. The boat rocked and flipped over, pitching us both into the lake."

She closed her eyes, her hands gripping his in her lap. For long moments she sat perfectly still. His heart ached for her. She roused and looked into his eyes. "I managed to climb onto the upturned boat and cling to it until help came. I called and called for Neville, but he had disappeared. They found him the next day, but they wouldn't let me see him. I wasn't even allowed to go to the funeral. My mother went into a decline and passed away not long after. My father has barely spoken to me since. He blames me for Neville's death, but no more than I blame myself."

She disengaged her hands. "So now you know my worst secret, Nick Kennedy. I killed my brother. If I hadn't been trying to best him, he'd still be alive today." An empty look came into her eyes, utter defeat.

He smoothed his palms down her upper arms and gripped her elbows. "Annie Fairfax, what utter nonsense. You were a child. Your brother's death was an accident. You were no more culpable in his death than I."

She shrugged his hands away. "If it wasn't my fault, then why does my father think it is? Why won't he talk to me? Why won't he love me?"

She rose and tried to brush past him, but he blocked her way. "Grief makes people do strange things. Maybe your father didn't know how to handle his sorrow. Maybe he didn't know how to treat a little girl who was also grieving. But Neville's death wasn't your fault. It was an accidental drowning. You have to stop blaming yourself."

"How?" The cry burst from her throat as if under pressure. "How can I not blame myself? Everyone who has ever loved me has blamed me for his death. My mother, my father, I think even Haze—" Her voice broke on a sob.

Nick brought her into his arms again. "Annie, those people are wrong. And you're wrong. Stop punishing yourself. If you don't, this will eat you alive." Guilt stabbed him.

What a hypocrite I am. I'm preaching what I don't practice. But this is different. I was a grown man, not a little girl trying to outdo her brother. I should've known better than to try that harbor run. I should've done something different. If I had, my crew would still be alive.

Annie relaxed in his arms, spent with emotion.

Nick cradled her against his chest for a moment, then stepped back a half pace. He took her face in his hands, using his thumbs to swipe away the last of her tears. He was all kinds of a fool, but he couldn't stop himself.

The instant Nick's lips settled on hers, Annie knew she'd been waiting for this moment for a long time. Clasped in his arms, sheltered, secure, she gave herself over to the wonder of his kiss. The salty taste of her tears mingled with the sweetness of knowing herself cherished by the man she'd come to care for so deeply. In that instant, she dreamed a thousand dreams, made a thousand plans, let her heart soar.

With the abruptness of being thrown in the lake, Nick broke the kiss and pushed her from him.

Annie blinked, stunned. Had she done something wrong?

His hands fisted at his sides, and his breath came in gasps. Those lips that had so recently caressed hers formed a hard line. He swallowed hard. "My apologies. I had no right to do that. It won't happen again, I assure you."

"Nick?" Her hand went out to him. "You don't need to apologize."

He shook his head, staring past her shoulder toward the lighthouse. "You have no idea, Annie. There are things that prevent me from—" He broke off and turned away from her. "I'm sorry." He strode across the clearing and disappeared into the watch room.

Annie sank to the fallen log and buried her face in her hands. Great sobs wracked her shoulders, sticking in her throat. She wiped her eyes once more with his handkerchief, noting the bold NNK embroidered in navy blue on the white linen. How could he be so kind and gallant on the one hand, and so cold and distant on the other?

She had bared her soul, her deepest shameful secret to him, had dared to dream he might be able to look past that and love her anyway; but in the end, she was as alone and unlovable as ever. And she had no one to blame but herself.

fifteen

"It's your turn, Annie." Clyde twirled his mallet like a baton.

Annie nodded and bent over her ball. How incongruous, to be playing croquet when the entire world had crashed to bits around her. Imogen and Ezra seemed oblivious, seated on the porch swing, rocking gently, shaded from the Sunday afternoon sun. Against her will, her eyes strayed to Nick. He stood beside the porch, arms crossed, staring past the lighthouse to the waves beyond. In the two days since he'd kissed her and walked away, he hadn't said a word to her.

His kiss. As she had done a thousand times, she allowed her mind to race back, to remember every second in his arms, the feel of his lips on hers. Then, like a bucket of lake water in the face, the cold shock of his dismissal struck her. She blamed herself. Her actions had been too emotional, too forward. She should've kept control, held her tongue and buried the truth about her brother's death. By baring her soul, she'd opened herself up for rejection.

For an hour after he left her in the clearing, Annie had cried out to God, opening places in her heart that she'd tried to keep hidden from Him. Broken, she laid it bare before Him. All her guilt, her feelings of abandonment, of loneliness, she brought out for Him to touch, to heal. She asked for and received forgiveness and peace.

With His forgiveness came the knowledge that she had to confess her identity to her employers. A great weight lifted from her when she determined to do the right thing. Though her heart ached for Nick, she felt cleansed and renewed. "Thank You, Father, for loving me in spite of who I am. Please give me the strength to do what You want me to do." Now she just needed to find a way to tell Imogen and

Ezra the truth about who she really was. And Nick. She'd have to confess to Nick one more of her secrets.

She whacked the ball, sending it well past the wicket. It rolled across the grass and came to rest under a hawthorn bush. If only she knew how to broach the subject with Nick, to apologize and somehow get their relationship on an even keel again.

Clyde rubbed his ear and sauntered over to her. "You all right, Miss Annie?"

She tried to smile but had a feeling she didn't pull it off too well. "I guess I'm just not in the mood to play today. I can't seem to concentrate."

He nodded then inclined his head toward Nick. "Like someone else. Guess he's got a lot on his mind these days waiting to see if the boom is going to be lowered for him poking Grover Dillon in the nose. Rotten luck him turning out to be the inspector's brother." Clyde took the mallet from her hand. "Nick's been touchier than a nest of wasps for a couple days now. Though I shouldn't complain. He's taken extra watches in the tower the past two nights."

So that's where Nick had been. Annie had missed him at mealtimes and especially in the evenings in the parlor. She hadn't been able to make herself ask after him. It mortified her that he would avoid her this way.

"I'll put the game away, Miss Annie. It's almost time for the sing-along."

"Thank you, Clyde. Maybe we can try again next Sunday." *If I'm still here next Sunday.* She mounted the steps to the porch and sank into a chair.

Imogen lay with her head back against the swing. Her mouth tensed in a line, patient forbearance stamped on her expression.

"Headache again?" Annie leaned forward and took Imogen's hand where it lay limp on the arm of the swing.

Imogen nodded, not opening her eyes. "Just a touch."

"Can I get you anything? Tea? A cold cloth?"

"Thank you, child. I'll just rest here. The fresh air helps."

Ezra looked up from his newspaper and frowned. "Perhaps we should cancel the sing-along today."

"Oh no, Ezra. I love the music." Imogen shifted and opened her dark eyes, entreating him. "And Clyde plays so well. Please?"

Ezra nodded, smiling, but eyes still clouded with worry.

Annie envied them their closeness, the assurance and security of their love for one another. Imogen, willing to brave being ill in this isolated spot so she could be with her husband. Ezra, doing all he could to make his wife happy, to ease her suffering as much as possible, allowing her to be here with him because that's what she wanted most. Just yesterday he'd come into the house with a bouquet of spring wildflowers, eager as a young suitor. And hadn't Imogen blushed like a bride at his attention?

Annie's gaze went to Nick again. He stood with his back to the porch, studying the west horizon. His white shirt stretched taut across his shoulders. She could see his face in three-quarter profile—the strong jaw, the dark brows, watchful eyes scanning the water. A fitful breeze gusted, blowing his hair and fluttering his sleeves. Though he stood no more than twenty feet away, the gulf between them yawned. She longed to go to him, to recapture the closeness of the past. But she couldn't risk his rejection again.

"Looks like some weather building in the northwest." Nick didn't turn around when he spoke.

Annie followed his gaze. A low smudge of gray hung in the sky, ominous, but far off. Another gust of air scurried past, whipping up puffs of dust from the path and bringing the smell of rain.

Ezra nodded. "It's been a quiet spring so far. We're due for a storm or two. Is the dingy in the boat shed?"

"All secure." Nick crossed his arms. "It will be a good

night to be inside, I think."

Clyde came up the walk from his quarters, guitar in his hand. He settled himself on the steps and strummed the strings. "Any requests?"

" 'It Is Well with My Soul.' " Imogen lay back again, her voice barely above a whisper.

Clyde's clear tenor drifted out. Annie lay back, allowing the music to soothe her rumpled spirits. As he sang of the great forgiveness that was hers through Christ, she relaxed, her heart unclenching. God's forgiveness was unconditional. He already knew her deepest secrets, and He loved her anyway. That would have to be enough.

She watched Nick through half-closed eyes. Though his actions had hurt her, she didn't blame him, not exactly. There could be no hope of a future together unless she told him who she really was. Would it make a difference? Would the fact that she was a wealthy heiress matter to him? The entire charade had become so burdensome, a barricade between her and the people she had come to care about. All at once the situation was intolerable. Annie sat up, resolved to come clean. She braced herself to rise. Nick deserved to know first, in private. She would apologize for her emotional display of two days ago and tell him the truth about running away from home. Then she would tell Imogen and Ezra. She owed them that much for their kindness to her.

A whistle blasted the air, freezing Annie in a half-standing position.

"That sounded like the *Marigold.*" Ezra bolted up, his paper falling to the porch floor in a rustling fan.

Imogen sat up, holding her hand to her head, squinting against the pain. "The *Marigold*? Isn't that just like Dillon, calling on a Sunday with a surprise inspection?"

Annie's heart turned to ice. The lighthouse tender. Inspector Dillon. She did a mental gallop through the house. The kitchen was spotless. Fresh cinnamon rolls sat on the counter under a cloth. Would he consider them a bribe? The kitchen inventory lists hung on a clipboard by the pantry door, as up to the minute as she could make them. And her room. He wouldn't recognize the place. Neat as a sheet. Bed made, belongings in the drawers, not a hint of dust, not even under the iron bedstead. She'd even washed the windows yesterday.

The group burst into activity. Nick and Clyde sprinted across the grass to their quarters to don their uniforms. Ezra scooped up the newspapers and thrust them into Annie's arms. He checked his buttons and cuffs while Imogen straightened the cushions and folded the afghan she'd used as a shawl.

Annie hurried inside to put the paper on the shelf in the parlor and to check her appearance in the mirror in the tiny hall. She repinned a few locks the breeze had displaced and made sure her blouse was neatly tucked into her skirt. She made a face at her reflection. If only the inspector had held off another half hour she might have been able to get Nick alone. At least she would have been able to confess her identity and get out from under this load of guilt.

At the door, she hesitated. Should she don her apron over her dress? No, not on a Sunday afternoon. Inspector Dillon would have to take her as she was.

When Annie stepped back onto the porch, Imogen took her hand. "The men have gone down to the dock. We'll wait here for them."

Annie's hands trembled. She took a deep, shuddering breath. *"The name of the Lord is a strong tower."* Lord, we're running to You. Keep us safe.

ಎ

Nick braced his legs apart and clasped his hands behind his back, never taking his eyes off the launch that bobbed toward the dock. The west wind shoved the waves before it into the shore, whitecaps crashing on the rocks, sucking and slurping under the dock beneath his feet. Storm clouds continued to build to the northwest, black and surly.

Ezra stood beside him. "You know I'll speak on your behalf to the inspector."

Nick shook his head. "Don't jeopardize your career for me. Sutton Island needs you. The Lighthouse Board needs you. Don't throw away a thirty-year career fighting with Jasper Dillon. I can take whatever he dishes out."

"That may be true, but I don't want to see you hung out to dry because of a personal matter. If Grover Dillon wasn't his brother, he would've read the report and put it out of his mind instead of showing up here to condemn you for it."

"Maybe he dislikes his brother and is here to give me a medal." Nick's lips twitched, and he cast Ezra a sidelong glance.

"This is no joking matter." Ezra frowned. "If he fires you, where will you go? Do you have funds to live on until you find another job? You know I'll give you a reference."

Guilt raced across the back of Nick's neck. He had more funds than Ezra Batson had seen in his lifetime. He had a name, power, finances, a share in the largest shipping company on the lake, not to mention a mansion and a family—all of which he'd turned his back on and hidden as if he was ashamed of them. But he wasn't ashamed of his family, only of himself.

"I'll be fine if he cuts me loose." But would he really? Being fired meant leaving the island, leaving Annie. The past two days had been horrible, wanting to go to her and tell all but knowing he had no right to. Knowing she would reject him if she knew who he was and what he had done. And how could he ask for her hand when, in truth, he was betrothed to another? The pain of knowing he'd hurt her, that she didn't understand why he had walked away, ground upon his soul. He longed to be free of the entanglements of his past so he could pursue and win her.

The launch neared the dock, and Clyde hurried out to

grab the lines and make her fast.

Inspector Dillon climbed out of the boat, belligerent expression in place, reminding Nick of a pugnacious rooster.

Nick forced himself to relax, to unclench his fists and loosen his jaw.

Dillon turned back to the boat and assisted a woman onto the dock. She stood no more than five feet tall, her face wrinkled, eyes bright. A bonnet covered most of her hair, but what Nick could see was pure white. He glanced at Ezra who shrugged and shook his head.

Leaving the woman to trail behind, Dillon strutted up the dock. Clyde lifted bags, presumably the woman's, and followed. The inspector stopped before them, scowling at Nick. His nose wrinkled as if he had encountered a foul smell.

"Inspector." Nick stepped forward.

Dillon looked him over from head to toe. "If you thought I wouldn't hear about your behavior, you are sadly mistaken. However, I have no intention of conducting business here on the dock with weather coming in. We'll discuss your situation in the house like civilized individuals." The words burst from him, as if he expected Nick to wrestle him to the ground and demand to know his punishment that moment. Dillon looked over their shoulders to where the path disappeared through the trees. "I see Miss Fairfax didn't come down to the dock. Well, I'll deal with her in good time as well." He motioned to the old woman. "This is Miss Thorpe. She'll be taking over Miss Fairfax's duties beginning today."

Nick's heart lurched. Annie was leaving the station?

Dillon smirked. Pompous little fool, swelled up with his own power. He needed a proper lesson—like a dunking in the lake.

Lord, help me keep my temper. And help Annie. She's going to be devastated.

"Is that really necessary?" Ezra smoothed his hands over

his brass buttons. "We have no complaints with Miss Fairfax. She's settled in quite well."

"You may have no complaints, Mr. Batson, but the Lighthouse Board feels differently."

"The Lighthouse Board or just you?" Nick's eyes narrowed.

Dillon's lips curled in scorn. "You are in no position to chide me, sir. I would suggest you concern yourself with your own situation. I'll concern myself with Miss Fairfax." He turned his back and started up through the trees.

Clyde shouldered past with the bags, eyes downcast, freckles standing out across his pale face. Nick stood aside to let him pass.

Ezra's brows came together, but he offered Miss Thorpe his arm to assist her up the steep path. "Welcome to Sutton Island, Miss Thorpe."

"Please, call me Hazel."

sixteen

Annie recognized the stooped figure instantly. Emotions clashed in her chest—homesickness so sharp she wanted to cry, regret that she hadn't been able to confess to Nick before he found out on his own who she was, resignation at her father sending Hazel to fetch her home, a tinge of anxiety at the welcome she would receive when she faced him.

She searched Nick's face for the disappointment she knew would be there. But he bore only a look of concern, his brows down, his eyes troubled.

Dillon sneered and puffed out his chest, small in stature, small in mind. Seeing him again left a stale taste in her mouth, and she found her lips tightening. He'd no doubt relish her unmasking. She braced herself for his unsavory comments.

"Miss Fairfax, this is your replacement, Miss Thorpe. I'm officially relieving you of your duties, effective immediately. Miss Thorpe is more than capable of running the household and assisting Mrs. Batson. You may pack your things. The ferry will pick you up tomorrow morning and return you to Duluth. You are no longer needed here."

Annie blinked.

Hazel stared hard at her, her eyes willing Annie to keep silent. Her former governess stepped forward, holding out her wrinkled hand. "Pleased to meet you, Miss Fairfax. I'm sure you'll be able to show me over the house and my duties before the morrow." Hazel gripped Annie's hand so hard Annie's knuckles popped.

She cleared her throat. "Miss Thorpe." The words came out strained. Annie now knew how the birds felt when they flew into the tower windows. Blinded, stunned, reeling.

Dillon mounted the stairs and swept the group with an imperious glare. "If the gentlemen will assemble in the parlor. You women won't be needed for our discussions."

"I'd like the ladies to be present." Nick's face was casual, but his voice held a challenging edge.

Dillon pursed his lips, his weedy mustache poking out. "Very well, but I warn you, this is not a social gathering." He swept into the house, his shoes squeaking on the polished floor.

Annie didn't know what to think.

Hazel pulled her down to whisper in her ear. "Not a word until we can talk."

Annie nodded, sure she couldn't speak even if she knew what to say. Her legs resembled wooden planks as she shuffled, stiff-kneed, into the house. Hazel was here, Annie had been fired, and now Nick's livelihood was on the chopping block. This day couldn't possibly get any worse.

❧

They filed into the parlor like a jury into a courtroom. Nick elected to stand by the fireplace, not wanting Inspector Dillon to look down at him. He'd take whatever the inspector had to say standing up.

Something about Annie's demeanor disturbed him. She kept darting glances at the new housekeeper as if she expected that lady to do something unpredictable. And Miss Thorpe missed nothing, her black eyes moving from face to face, studying, evaluating. He doubted anyone could fool Miss Thorpe for long.

Dillon sat in the wingback chair and placed his feet primly side by side, withdrawing a sheaf of papers from an inner pocket. He perched a pair of glasses on his narrow nose and studied the pages, though Nick was sure the inspector knew the contents by heart.

The silence stretched.

Clyde coughed and dug for his handkerchief, snorting

loudly. "Sorry," he muttered, stuffing the red cloth back into his hip pocket.

"Mr. Batson, I am here to inform you that I shall be making further changes to your staff effective immediately. This man"—he gestured toward Nick—"has been deemed unsuitable as an employee of the Lighthouse Board."

Ezra straightened. "Mr. Dillon, Nick is an exemplary worker, and his character is of the highest quality. I agree that in this one instance he might've chosen a better way to express his opinion, but he had considerable provocation. Your brother was quite drunk and belligerent."

Nick winced. *Don't do it, Ezra. Think of your career.*

Dillon scowled. "Mr. Batson, I have reviewed the incident fully. While my brother's actions were regrettable, this man had no right to assault him. That sort of behavior is unworthy of an employee of the Lighthouse Board. But that is not why he is being released. You say his character is above reproach? I beg to differ."

Nick's gut clenched. A terrible sense of foreboding swept through him, leaving him weak and unsettled.

A sneer spread across the inspector's face. "This man has been lying to you from the day you met him. He obtained this position under false pretenses. The man you know as Nick Kennedy is, in truth, Noah Kennebrae, disgraced captain of the ship *Bethany*. If I had known his identity when he applied for employment, I never would've hired him. He knew this and lied to gain this position."

Shame thrust up in Nick's chest. He looked from one face to another.

Ezra and Imogen regarded him with shock. Clyde with stunned awe. Dillon bared his teeth in a feral smile of triumph. But Annie, the one he cared the most about, sat like a stone, face pale, eyes wide.

"Annie, I—" He what? How could he explain to her?

Dillon tapped the papers on his knee then put the last nail

in Nick's coffin. "Mr. Kennebrae, now would be a good time for you to return to Duluth. I spoke with your grandfather just yesterday. He informs me that your betrothal is on the verge of being announced in the papers. No doubt your bride will wish you to attend your own engagement party. She must be most anxious for your return."

Grandfather! Nick grimaced. He should've known the old man wouldn't take his defection lying down. But to announce the engagement in the papers? Without even knowing where Nick was? No, Abraham Kennebrae wouldn't do that. Jonathan must've told Grandfather where Nick had gone. His fists tightened. He'd have a word or two for his older brother when they met again.

A sob caught his ear. Annie rose, her eyes wide and accusing. "Engaged?" She blinked, sending a tear cascading down her cheek. "You're engaged to be married?" Without waiting for an answer, she fled, shoulders shaking, head bent.

Dillon rose, snickering. "Well, it seems your betrothal comes as a shock to the young lady. Just what sort of relationship do you have with the girl? Perhaps it is best both of you are leaving the island. The Lighthouse Board will not tolerate loose morals amongst its workforce."

Nick's hands shot out and grabbed Dillon by the lapels. He hauled the shorter man up until he stood on tiptoe.

Blood drained from Dillon's face, his eyes stretching open until white showed all the way around his irises.

Nick towered over him, panting. "How dare you besmirch that girl's character! She's as innocent and pure as spring rain. Don't judge everyone by your low standards, you guttersnipe." He shook the inspector. "You've waltzed in here, eager to hurt and ruin and destroy. Well, you've accomplished your mission. But know this, if you ever cross my path again, if you ever utter one word against Annie Fairfax, I'll see you pay for it. I'll throw every bit of influence the Kennebrae name has behind seeing you ruined and thrown out of the Lighthouse Service." Nick released his grasp, and Dillon fell back in the chair in a heap. Nick's hand shook with the urge to haul the petty little man upright again and punch him as he had the drunken captain.

Ezra stepped between them, putting his hands on Nick's upper arms. "No more, son. You've defended her honor. Anything more would be wrong."

For a long moment, Nick stood still, muscles tense, pulse throbbing. Then his head dropped, his shoulders sagging. He had to go after Annie, to try to explain. If only he'd come clean two days ago instead of walking away from her.

Lord, I know I shouldn't ask You for help getting out of my own tangled lies, but if You could please help me find a way out of this, a way of telling Annie the truth, I'd be grateful.

He headed into the kitchen. A gust of wind caught the screen door, yanking it open then whipping it shut with a *crack*. With quick steps he crossed the floor to stick his head outside. A gust pushed against his face, chill and moist, a precursor to rain. Black clouds tumbled overhead, darkening the sky. Annie would have to wait. He started toward the tower. With inclement weather rolling in, he must get the lamps lit.

His footsteps clanged on the metal stairs. He jogged upwards, eager to do his duty and then find Annie. Though his hands raced, pumping the fuel tanks, checking the gauges, lighting the kerosene wicks, his mind raced faster. What could he say to her? How could he make her understand about his grandfather and his family and the loss of his ship which prompted his escape in the first place? Would she listen to him? Would she understand?

The lamps flared to life, momentarily blinding him as he shut the panel and ducked out from under the lens. He hustled down the stairs to release the pin holding the chained weights. The lantern began to revolve. Nick blinked, grasping his watch to check the timing. Perfect. Ironic, that. Everything in his life had exploded into chaos, but the light mechanisms rolled on.

He stepped outside the watch room and from habit scanned the lake. The dark hulk of a freighter plowed through the rising waves. Nick grabbed a pair of field glasses from the hook inside the door and held them to his eyes. No name showed on the bows. Every inch of the ship gleamed with new paint. She bucked, her nose slewing a bit. Why didn't her captain straighten her out to face the waves instead of taking them quarterways? If the storm broke in a fury, the boat could swamp, or worse, roll completely over.

Nick jerked the glasses down. He didn't have time for this. He had to find Annie. Before he could return the binoculars to their hook, a distress whistle pierced the stormy air.

seventeen

Morse flashes began from the pilothouse. Nick grabbed a pencil and paper from the watch room desk and began transcribing the signals.

> CAPTAIN INJURED. MUST REACH DULUTH QUICKLY.
> NEED YOUR HELP, NOAH. WILL SEND LAUNCH. ELI.
> CAPTAIN INJURED. MUST REACH DULUTH QUICKLY.
> NEED YOUR HELP, NOAH. WILL SEND LAUNCH. ELI.
> CAPTAIN—

Nick quit transcribing, the pencil falling to the grass. Eli was on that ship? And he knew Nick was on Sutton Island? The distress whistle pierced the air again.

Clyde and Ezra hurried around the corner of the watch room. "What is it?"

Nick held out the paper to Ezra. "It's my brother. They need help."

Ezra scanned the page. "Clyde, you're on the watch. Make the proper journal notation. Nick, er, Noah? I hardly know what to call you. Captain Kennebrae?" He stared intently at Nick's face.

Familiar guilt pierced Nick's chest at the mention of his former title. All the doubt, the pain, the shame he'd been running from for months crowded back, rooting him to the spot.

Captain.

He couldn't go, couldn't step onto the deck and assume command ever again. He couldn't run the risk of making another mistake, of taking the lives of innocent crewmen.

Ezra peered through the glasses. "They're putting out a

launch. Water's getting wild out there."

A fat raindrop pelted Nick's cheek. The cold water startled him, shaking him to life. "What does he think I can do?"

"You can get that ship into the harbor safely."

Nick studied the ship. A brand new boat, probably only a skeleton crew aboard. With the captain out of action, there likely wasn't another crewman aboard who could take a ship into Duluth in a storm. Especially riding light and getting kicked around in a wind that would only worsen as the storm rolled over.

"You have to go, son." Ezra lowered the glasses. "You're the only one who can help them."

Still Nick stood, rain falling faster. He couldn't do it. And yet, if he didn't, wouldn't he be condemned anyway? *God, what are You trying to do to me?* "I'll go. Have Clyde pack my gear on the ferry tomorrow." He thrust out his hand. "I know I have a lot of explaining to do, and if I had time I would. For now, know that I appreciate everything you've done for me and that I regret deceiving you."

Ezra shook his hand, looking him square in the eyes. "Son, I can guess at your reasons. And I don't hold anything against you. Your brother needs your help. Get down to the dock quick now, and go with God."

"Signal the ship that I'll meet the launch." Nick tossed the words back over his shoulder as he headed for the path to the water. "And tell Annie I'm sorry."

❧

Annie stood beside the window of her bedroom, arms crossed at her waist, head leaning against the curtains. Raindrops streamed down the panes, making the trees and buildings outside watery blobs of color. Every ten seconds the beacon swept overhead, its light shaft spearing the downpour.

No wonder he walked away from me. He's got a fiancée in Duluth.

What was she like? Was she beautiful? Nick. . .no, Noah—

she must think of him as Noah Kennebrae now—was returning to his family to marry someone else. Another tear slipped down her cheek.

At least she hadn't broken down and told him her own identity. He never would've believed her. Here she was running from an engagement set up by her father, straight into the arms of a man who had a woman he loved back in Duluth. Of all the idiotic things to do. Why hadn't Ni—Noah told her? She never would've dreamed such fanciful, impossible dreams about him if she'd known he was in love with someone else.

Someone tapped on the door. She didn't answer. She didn't want to talk to anyone, especially not Noah Kennebrae.

The door opened. "Annie, child." Hazel.

Annie stood still. She'd grown up enough in the past six weeks to resist the urge to throw herself into Hazel's comforting arms and let her governess soothe away some of the hurt. A hard lump formed in Annie's throat.

"Anastasia, stop pouting and listen to me. I didn't come all this way for you to ignore me." Hazel's sharp, familiar tone forced Annie to turn around, but she kept her arms crossed in a defiant gesture. "Now sit down and let me talk."

Annie walked to the end of the bed and sat, pressing her hip into the footboard.

Hazel took the chair beside the dresser and positioned it so she could sit face-to-face with Annie. She eased her small body down.

"Child, I've regretted helping you leave Michaelton House since the moment you escaped. I've wrestled with my Lord and with my conscience every day. I had no right to help you defy your father, and I'm guilty of lying to him. But no more. I know you won't like it, but I've told him exactly where you are. I contacted Jasper Dillon and arranged to take your place. Jasper doesn't know who you are, and that's just the way your father wants it. Mercy, was he angry." She rolled her eyes and shook her head. "They've had the police looking for you and everything. I could hardly stand not telling them you were all right. Your father was so worried about you. I couldn't have him fearing the worst, and I couldn't stand lying to him anymore."

Lies. Everywhere lies. Annie let her hands fall to her lap. She was so tired of the lies. "It's all right, Hazel. You know, just this afternoon I screwed up my courage to come clean, to tell everyone here who I was. I guess it doesn't matter now. The one person I really wanted to tell was hiding secrets of his own."

Hazel's dark eyes searched Annie's face. "Just what do you feel for that man, Noah Kennebrae?"

The sound of his name made prickles of shame race up her arms. "I don't feel anything for Noah Kennebrae. I thought I loved Nick Kennedy though." Her voice came out in a whisper. "I did love him."

Hazel crossed the room and sat beside Annie. Her thin, old arms came around Annie's shoulders. "Annie, girl, I'm sorry. I wish I'd never gone along with helping you escape. I didn't think of all the trouble it would cause. Your father is sending a launch for you in the morning. He didn't want you on the ferry for fear someone might recognize you and ask awkward questions. He'll meet you in the harbor as soon as you dock. Do exactly as he says. He's going to bluster at you, but trust me, he loves you and he was worried about you. Things will turn out for the best. Just trust me."

"Trust you? Trust isn't coming easy these days. I can't even trust myself."

"Well, if you can't trust me, then trust the Good Lord. He knows what is best for you, and He says to obey your father. Have a little faith."

Annie said no more. She had never felt so alone, so abandoned before. Even Hazel had taken her father's part. But it didn't matter anymore. She'd lost Nick forever. Without him, she might as well fall in line with whatever future her father had planned.

❧

Nick met the dingy at the dock and hopped aboard without even waiting for them to tie up. Now that he'd made the decision to go, he wanted to get there as quickly as possible. Rain lashed his face; spray kicked up before the bow of the launch, splashing into the boat. The two-man crew fought to keep the craft pointed into the waves. Nick grabbed a bucket and bailed the water sloshing around his boots.

The ship lurched on the rough seas, bobbing as the surf increased. Lightning split the sky, followed by a *boom* of thunder. Nick ducked instinctively. The clouds opened. He swiped the water from his eyes and shivered. Even in early June, the storm chilled to the bone. His mind balked at what he was about to do, but his heart had no choice. Not when his brother, his twin, needed him.

The small boat pulled alongside the freighter, the boats crashing together. A rope ladder flopped over the side. Nick grabbed the wet hemp, his boot slipping on the soaked wooden rung. A wave slapped the side of the freighter, dousing him with icy lake water. His teeth clattered together.

Hands reached down from the railing above and grabbed his shoulders and arms, heaving him onto the deck. Around him, ropes were hurled down to the men in the launch to make fast so the small craft could be winched aloft and lashed to the deck.

Nick clung to the rail, getting his sea legs, then made his way to the pilothouse. Warm light showed in fuzzy, rain-smeared halos from the windows. He couldn't help but notice that this ship was designed exactly like the *Bethany*, from the pilothouse to the deck to the smokestack. Horrible feelings of déjà vu swept over him. Familiar, terrible, walking-through-his-own-nightmare feelings.

Eli met him at the pilothouse door. His brother—younger

by twenty-three minutes—grabbed him by the shoulders and pulled him into a mighty hug. Relief etched his features. "I can't tell you how glad I am to see you. We're in a mess."

And Nick was supposed to get them out of it? His stomach roiled, weakness radiating out from his middle and draining his limbs of strength. What was he doing here?

Eli pulled him into the pilothouse.

A gust of warmth hit Nick's face. Steam heat. Water dripped from his clothes onto the floor. Everything was just the same—the pilothouse, the chart room behind, the brass chadburn, all exactly like the *Bethany*.

"Get out of that wet jacket. Here, put this on." Eli swept a coat off a hook beside the door to the chart room.

Nick shucked the sodden garment and shouldered into the rough, dry wool coat Eli handed him. In the center of the pilothouse, behind and to the right of the wheel and helmsman, the captain's chair stood bolted to the floor. Nick averted his eyes. He couldn't sit there. He couldn't let these men place their lives in his hands. "Where's the captain?" Perhaps the injury wasn't too bad. Perhaps the captain would be here soon to take over.

"We put him in his cabin. He slipped going down the ladder into the engine room and hit his head. Bled like crazy and he hasn't woken up. I think he broke some ribs in the fall, too. The cook is sitting with him. He needs more doctoring than we can give him."

The helmsman gripped the wheel, brow scrunched, face pale. The ship took another broadside wave and rolled.

Nick grabbed the back of the captain's chair, bracing himself. "Helm, ten degrees right rudder." He hadn't meant to bark the order, but the words forced their way out of his throat. "All ahead two-thirds." His hand grasped the cold brass handle of the chadburn, and he dialed down to the engine room for more power. "Keep the bow pointed into the waves." The mantle of command crowded about him with uneasy familiarity.

Eli clapped him on the back. "Boy, am I glad you answered my call."

"What are you doing on the lake in a green boat with a skeleton crew? I thought you were in Virginia."

Eli braced against the pitch of the hull. "She's the *Kennebrae Siloam*, fresh off the ways of the shipyard. Grandfather cabled me to pick her up in Detroit on the way home and get back to Duluth on the double. Said I couldn't miss your engagement party. He's still sore I didn't make it back for Jonathan's wedding. The question is what are you doing on Sutton Island?"

Noah shook his head. Grandfather's scheming was another thing he'd have to deal with, but not now. "Later." He tapped the helmsman on the shoulder. "Straighten out that bow and stop looking at the compass. The pull of the iron ranges throws the compass off course. Keep your eyes peeled for the Two Harbors light. Even in these conditions, you should be able to pick it up fairly soon." Like they had that fateful night last November. He should've tried the turn into Two Harbors instead of running for Duluth. Then maybe his men wouldn't have perished.

Lord, I can't do this. Why have You brought me back here to this place? Why have You put another crew's fate in my hands?

To take his mind off his reeling thoughts, he turned to Eli. "I suppose Jonathan told you where I was?"

Eli braced his legs and held onto the rail running under the pilothouse windows. "Don't be sore at Jonathan. He was all set to come get you himself a month ago, but Grandfather told him to wait. Something about the wedding plans being on hold and Sutton Island being as good a place as any for you to wait. Jonathan's letter wasn't all that clear."

"I'll bet." Noah rubbed his face.

"Sir?" The helmsman gripped the wheel, holding it hard against the force of the wind and waves. "Will we be trying to make Two Harbors?"

At that moment another scalding shaft of lightning arced across the sky. Noah blinked against the black spots hovering in his view.

Eli spoke up, "The captain needs doctoring, but I think Duluth is his best chance. I'm not even sure if there is a doctor in Two Harbors."

Memories swamped Noah. The *Bethany* bucking and heaving in the storm. The decision not to try to make the turn into Two Harbors. Jonathan's face, so pale. Everyone relying on Noah to know what to do. He swallowed hard. "How many crew members aboard?"

"Eight, counting the cook. Two stokers—they came to get you in the launch—two deckhands, an engineer, the helmsman, the cook, and the captain. Then there's you and me." Eli ticked them off on his fingers. "Ten, all together. And, Noah, we're light on fuel. With no load and a quick run from Detroit to Duluth, they didn't top up the coal bunkers."

A hollow pit Noah had been trying to ignore swelled in his middle. Low on fuel, green boat, skeleton crew, huge storm. If the captain downstairs wasn't in such dire need of medical attention, the smart thing to do would be to drop anchor and ride out the storm, maintaining just enough power to keep them headed into the waves. Noah tugged on his bottom lip, wishing he had his whiskers back to rub while he thought.

"Call everyone to the pilothouse."

eighteen

Men crowded the bridge. The cook elected to remain below with the captain. Every face regarded Noah solemnly. The helmsman continued at his position, the others lined the walls of the small room.

"Men, there's no sugarcoating the situation. The safest course is to drop anchor and wait out the storm. You all know the risks of attempting a harbor run in rough seas. The captain is in a bad way. I don't know if he's going to make it, but his chances are better if we can get him to a doctor."

One of the crewmen, a grizzled man with enormous white side-whiskers, shifted a plug of tobacco in his mouth. "I say we risk it. I been with the cap'n for nigh onto twelve years now, and he deserves a chance." Several voiced their agreement.

Noah nodded. "We're riding light with no load. Fuel's low, so we have to commit one way or the other soon. Either we shut down all but the bare minimum and ride things out or we pile on the coal and get to Duluth as quickly as possible. You all know me, you know what happened the last time I captained a ship in a storm." He braced himself, but not one crewmember cast him a reviling glance. "But I'm willing to try to get us into the harbor."

Eli clasped him on the shoulder. "Noah, you're the best captain on the lake, and these men know it. We'll do everything we can to help you."

Fear churned in Noah, hot and cold by turns. Their faith humbled him. "Very well. Stokers, get down to the boilers and get to work." He turned to the engineer. "Throw her wide open. You and you, you're the deckhands, right?" Two narrow, lean men nodded, their slickers dripping water. "One of you get downstairs and relieve the cook and tell him to make sandwiches and coffee, lots of coffee. The other will stand by to relay messages and carry the food to the crew."

"What shall I do, Noah?" Eli raised his brows.

"Stay here and watch with the glasses. Daylight's fading. The instant you spot the harbor light, give a shout. I'll be watching, too." Noah settled into the captain's chair and gripped the arms. "And all of you, pray."

The men dispersed to their stations.

In less than five minutes the ship surged ahead, the engine throbbing. Waves broke over the bow, sending water pouring over the deck. With no cargo, the ship bobbed like an empty bottle on the waves. Noah braced himself for each roll.

Eli clung with one hand to the window frame, the other pressing the glasses to his eyes. "Awfully hard to see anything. The sky and the water are starting to merge."

Nick nodded. "It will get worse before it gets better." Images of the *Bethany*, of the storm, the faces of his crew members, flashed in his head. He second-guessed his decision a hundred times. What if he failed? What if history repeated itself and he lost another ship?

He thrust the thoughts aside. For the sake of the man lying injured on the bunk below, the crew would risk the narrow harbor entrance. For the captain's sake and his own, Noah would return to Duluth and all he'd fled two months ago.

"What did Jonathan say about the engagement?" He didn't really want to know, but it gave him something else to think about.

Eli shrugged. "Just that it would be in the papers by the end of the week. Noah Kennebrae to wed the daughter of Phillip Michaels."

"Michaels? The iron tycoon Michaels?" Noah remembered seeing his name on a few Kennebrae manifests, but most of his ore was handled by their archrival, Gervase Fox's company, Keystone Steel. "So, Grandfather plans to get all of the Michaels shipping contracts, does he?"

"Yeah, didn't he tell you who the girl was?"

"I didn't discuss it with him. I guess I didn't want to know. Maybe I thought if I ignored it, the problem would go away." How foolish. By stepping out of the discussion, he'd done nothing but give Grandfather a free hand.

"The Michaels's business would certainly keep the fleet busy. Between the grain from Jonathan's marriage and the ore from yours, we'll need half as many ships again to cover the contracts. Which will give me the perfect opportunity to test out my new ship design." The pilothouse lurched, rolling as a wave caught her off the port side.

"Don't get ahead of yourself there. I'm not marrying the Michaels heiress."

Eli whipped around. "That's not what Grandfather says. How're you going to get out of it?"

"I'll just tell Grandfather I'm in love with someone else, and I intend to marry her." *If she'll have me. If she can forgive me. And if I can find her again once she's left Sutton Island.* His heart thudded thickly in his throat. His beautiful Annie. He hadn't even gotten to say good-bye. As soon as he confronted his grandfather and this girl he was supposed to wed, he would begin his search.

Eli grinned. "In love with someone else? Who is she? And boy, is Grandfather going to be surprised. I can't wait to see what he says. That should be some show."

"I wouldn't be so complacent if I were you. He might just have you take my place with this Michaels girl."

Eli shook his head. "I'm married to my work. Grandfather will have to accept that. I wouldn't give up shipbuilding to marry any woman."

"Eli, you've never been in love. That's your trouble. If you had, you'd give up anything, any dream, any hope, to win the woman you love." The ache around Noah's heart intensified. He had to find Annie, to make her understand how much he loved her. And he had to get free of his grandfather's entanglements.

"Two Harbors Light, sir."

Noah's jaw tightened. He could play it safe and swing the boat into the security of Agate Bay. He could dodge the gauntlet of the Duluth ship channel. But the injured captain needed a doctor in Duluth.

The helmsman flicked a questioning glance his way.

"All ahead full, helm." The light at Two Harbors slid by on their starboard side. No turning back now.

The ship pitched and plowed through the waves for what seemed an eternity before a faint glow appeared through the gloom ahead.

"Duluth Harbor Light, sir." The helmsman peered through the window.

Noah tensed. "Left rudder five degrees. Line up on the starboard light. Bring her around." *Lord, help us. You promised to be a strong tower. We need that strength now.*

Several ships lay at anchor beyond the channel, riding out the storm before trying to enter the docks. Noah scanned the shoreline. The *Bethany* no longer lay broken on the shoal just outside the piers. He could be grateful for that at least.

Waves thrashed the piers, spewing up gray white foam, surging over the seawall higher than a man's head. The *Kennebrae Siloam* bucked and heaved, her nose plowing the water, targeting the window formed by the transport bridge.

"Reduce power." Noah's mouth went dry. He had little recollection of the *Bethany*'s wreck, having been tossed to the floor and rendered unconscious when she bottomed out in the channel. But what he'd awakened to was something he had no desire to relive. "Correct your course, helm. Waves hitting three-quarter on the port bow. Steady at the wheel."

Eli moved to stand behind Noah, holding the back of the captain's chair just as Jonathan had done seven months before.

Noah's hands ached from gripping the arms of the chair.

The bridge loomed ahead. Green water heaved against the bows. Lightning streaked the sky, precursor to a clap of thunder that shuddered through the steel hull and rattled the panes of the pilothouse.

The nose of the ship entered the canal. Rain ran down the windows. The green light of the pier lighthouse bathed the ship momentarily in an eerie light.

Noah could barely breathe. "Steady, helm." A heavy wave smacked the ship mid keel. She slewed, kicking the stern toward the pier. "Watch the cross current as soon as she noses through the channel."

The helmsman hung on as the ship bucked, spinning the wheel to edge the nose toward the starboard pier and bring the stern back in line. He wasn't quick enough, and the stern bounced off the steel and concrete pier, the impact vibrating through the ship.

For a moment, Noah closed his eyes, certain a repeat of the *Bethany* disaster was about to occur.

Eli grabbed Noah's shoulder.

Noah's eyes popped open. He dialed the chadburn, asking the engineer for more power. A rumble shot through the ship as the pistons responded to the increased steam from the boiler. The ship surged forward, scraping momentarily against the pier but righting herself and leaping under the bridge supports.

"You did it!" Eli grinned and punched Noah's arm. "I knew you could."

Noah brushed his brother's praise aside. "Signal the tugs. Take us into any empty Kennebrae dock and signal that we require medical assistance."

"Aye, aye, Captain Kennebrae."

Captain Kennebrae. A bittersweet homecoming indeed.

&

Two hours later, Noah shouldered through the doors of

Kennebrae House into the foyer, stripping off his coat as he went. Carved oak pillars stretched to his right and left down the grand hall, and overhead crystal chandeliers winked. The imposing staircase dominated the space, curving off on either hand to the balcony above. The sound of cutlery and china clinking drifted from the dining room at the end of the house.

The butler took his coat, eyes bright with welcome. "Mr. Noah. It is good to have you home, sir." The seasoned servant concealed whatever surprise he might have felt at Noah's appearance behind a long-practiced mask of imperturbability. Some things never changed.

"McKay, is Grandfather at supper?"

Eli shoved his way in the front door. He dropped bags, coat, and an armful of chart papers in a heap on the marble mosaic of the entryway. "McKay! Now I know I'm home." Ignoring protocol, he wrapped the butler in a bear hug.

"Mr. Eli, it's been too long, sir."

"That it has. And I brought the prodigal home with me." Eli flashed a boyish grin. "Or maybe he brought me home. We had to make a harbor run in the dark in the teeth of this storm." As if to punctuate his words, lightning flashed through the stained glass windows above the landing before them, bringing to colorful life the lotus blossoms and birds held captive in the leaded design. The thick walls and slate roof of Kennebrae House muffled the thunder to a distant roar.

McKay motioned for them to follow him toward the dining room.

"Mr. Noah and Mr. Eli, sir." He announced them and withdrew.

Massive silver candelabra graced the mahogany table. In the flickering candlelight, Grandfather's dark eyes gleamed but registered no surprise.

Jonathan rose from his position at Grandfather's right

hand, a smile splitting his normally sober expression. "Noah, Eli, welcome home." Jonathan advanced to shake hands with them. His eyes studied Noah's face. "I had no idea you were coming home tonight."

Melissa pushed back her chair and joined them, kissing Noah on the cheek. "Welcome home, Noah." Her face held questions and compassion in equal measure. She squeezed his arm. "I'm glad you're back. I've missed you." She turned to Eli. "And you must be Eli. It is so good to meet you at last."

Eli grinned. "Johnny, old boy, you sure came out the winner catching this gal. Melissa, Grandfather sent me a copy of your wedding photo. Your picture doesn't do you justice. You are loveliness itself." He kissed her warmly on the cheek and hugged her. "Too bad I wasn't here at the time. I'd have snatched you up before Jonathan knew what hit him."

Jonathan cocked an eyebrow at Eli who stalked around the table to greet Grandfather.

Noah braced himself for battle and followed.

Grandfather sat straight in his chair. Gaslight from the wall sconces ran along the metal arcs on his wheelchair. His snowy hair lay like a helmet on his large head. The Kennebrae tartan blanket in his lap covered his stick-thin legs. Everything Noah loved and everything he resented about this man clashed in his breast.

"Noah, Eli, I'm pleased you've returned. Sit down, have some dinner." Grandfather motioned to the discreet screen in the corner beside the silver hutch.

A maid's white cap bobbed, and she disappeared into the kitchen.

"I was just about to tell Jonathan and Melissa about the party tomorrow night at Michaelton House."

Eli pulled out a chair beside Melissa, leaving Noah to sit beside Jonathan. "Party? What a nice homecoming." McKay set a plate before him and placed cutlery and glasses. Eli dug into the meal as if he hadn't eaten in a week.

When the butler set food before him, Noah's gut churned and tightened.

"Though it is nice that your homecoming coincided with Noah's, the party is intended to announce and celebrate Noah's engagement." Grandfather took up his glass and sipped, staring at Noah with a challenge in his eyes.

Noah stared at his plate for a moment then raised his chin. "Grandfather, I have no intention of going through with this marriage. I won't put myself or some girl through it. Call off the party, extend my regrets, and get this notion out of your head."

Jonathan turned to Noah. "Noah, you don't have to call things off. I know you were upset when you left, but I have some news for you that might change things. We hauled the *Bethany* into dry dock and the engineers have been going over her."

Noah braced himself to hear what he already knew.

"We've conducted interviews with the remaining crew, and we've had two independent shipbuilders go over her. The wealth of evidence states that you made the only choice you could under those circumstances." Jonathan's gaze pierced Noah.

Noah leaned forward, his hands gripping his knife and fork.

Jonathan continued. "You remember how she was listing even before she hit the canal wall? The engineers say part of her hull had buckled and was taking on water. You had no choice but to attempt the harbor run. If you had laid out at anchor, she'd have gone down in a matter of an hour or so." He grinned broadly. "Everyone agrees that you saved our lives. Though some were lost, and we grieve for them and their families, more were rescued. You can stop blaming yourself. The *Bethany* will be out of commission for a while, but she'll be back on the lake next spring, maybe even this fall. You're not a failure. You're a hero. In fact, a reporter from the Duluth paper was at the shipyard today to hear the verdict. It will be all over town by tomorrow that you deserve the highest praise."

"Here, here." Eli raised his water glass. "I knew it. And you saved our necks today. This hero gambit is getting to be quite a habit with you."

Noah sat in stunned silence, processing Jonathan's words. For so long he'd assumed he'd made the wrong choice, that he'd jeopardized his crew. Could his brother's words be true? Had he made the right decision? Relief, questions, absolution, all crowded his mind.

"I'd like to go look at her when I have a chance." He forced the words through his thick throat. After he found Annie. Everything else was second to that. Surely she'd be aboard the *Jenny Klamath* when it returned to Duluth. He'd meet her at the dock tomorrow and confess everything.

"Me, too," Eli agreed. "And I want to talk to you, Grandfather, about implementing some of my new designs. The *Bethany* refit would be just the opportunity I need to try them out."

Grandfather nodded, his fingers steepled beneath his chin. "Good idea. Go tomorrow. Just be back here in time to leave for the party."

Noah's shoulders sagged. "I told you, Grandfather, I'm not getting married, at least not to the Michaels girl."

Grandfather's fingers fisted and he banged the table. "You will. The contracts are ready. Philip Michaels has already signed. The invitations to the party went out last week."

Noah narrowed his eyes. "Last week? But you didn't even know I'd be back in town. Or did you?"

The old man's chin lifted. "I knew it. I planned it. How do you think that unctuous little inspector knew your real name? When those ferry passengers you rescued returned to town, one of them came to see me. He recognized you as the captain of the *Bethany*, but you were using a different name. That's when I contacted the Lighthouse Board and let them know they had an imposter in their ranks. I knew they'd fire you and you'd be back here within the week."

"You had me fired?" Noah pushed his chair back.

"I wanted you home." Grandfather's back straightened. "I wanted you to stop running from your responsibilities. Now you're here, and you're exonerated from any wrongdoing regarding the *Bethany*. You're free to marry."

Noah stood. "When will you stop manipulating people? I'm not a chess piece for you to shove around and use to conquer your opposition. I have no intention of marrying this Michaels girl. Cancel the party, inform her family, and leave me alone. You don't have the hold over me that you had over Jonathan, though I'm pleased at how that all turned out."

He nodded toward Melissa, who smiled softly in return.

"I've proven these past two months that I can take care of myself. I'm not afraid to walk away from all this." He waved his hand toward the ornate room. "In truth, my heart belongs to another. I have every intention of marrying her when I find her again."

Grandfather scowled and tossed his napkin down. "Don't be a fool. Think of what your marriage would mean to the company, to Eli, who is filled to bursting with new shipbuilding ideas. If you marry into the Michaels family, we'll need at least six new ships, probably ten, to carry their ore. If you won't do it for yourself, then do it for your family. And who is this girl you say you love? Is she wealthy?"

"She's as poor as a fishwife, but I don't care. I'm not marrying her for money."

Noah regarded each of them—Grandfather, imperious and demanding; Jonathan, sober, staring at his hands in his lap; Eli, eager-eyed, chewing thoughtfully. And Melissa, her blue eyes filled with compassion.

Jonathan cleared his throat. "Don't blackmail him, Grandfather. Noah should marry for love. If he loves another, he should be free to pursue her."

Grandfather wheeled his chair back, expression dark. "Well, I'm not going to do his dirty work for him if he's as ungrateful as that for all the work I've done. He owes the girl and her family an explanation. He should at least meet his fiancée before he ruins her character by refusing to marry her."

Melissa nodded. "Noah, I don't deny you should have the right to marry whomever you choose, and I wish you success in winning the girl you say you love. But having been in this situation myself"—she smiled at Jonathan—"I know I would've been devastated and ashamed if I'd heard second-hand that my fiancé had broken the engagement. Please, at least meet the girl and tell her yourself. She might be grateful, and she might even be sympathetic to your cause."

Eli swallowed his last bite. "What about the party?"

Melissa's mouth firmed up. "If the invitations to a party have already gone out, it's too late to call things off." She turned to Grandfather who still fumed, glaring at Noah. "I wish you had informed me before now. I would've offered to help with the preparations."

"Don't be daft." He cleared his throat and softened his tone. "Michaels has it under control, I'm sure. I wanted it to be a surprise. You shouldn't be working so hard, not in your condition." His voice softened. "You have to take care of yourself."

A delicate blush colored her cheeks, and her eyes went soft.

Jonathan stood and placed his hand on her shoulder. "Noah, Eli, you can be the first to congratulate us. Another Kennebrae will join us late this fall."

Eli surged to his feet and enveloped Melissa in a hug.

Noah offered his congratulations, but his mind seethed against his grandfather.

"I can't believe you would do this to your family, Noah. My reputation is on the line, millions of dollars at stake, and you're just thinking about yourself." Grandfather wheeled himself from the room.

Jonathan shook his head. "Don't worry about it, Noah. You know how he is. He'll get over it."

Noah shook his head. "I wish I could do as he wants, but I can't. I can't marry someone when I love another." He imagined Annie's face when he met her at the dock. His lips twitched. Perhaps he should wear an old pair of boots.

nineteen

Annie gathered her belongings around her. What would her father say? At least the trip had been smooth, all traces of the previous day's storm washed away. The *Genevieve*, the private yacht of one of her father's friends—at least that's what one of the crew told her before showing her to the forward salon and shutting her inside—slid through the channel, the gulls dipping and wheeling around the steel girders of the bridge.

Had Hazel given Imogen Annie's letter explaining everything? Would Imogen, so kind and gentle, be able to forgive Annie for deceiving her? Would Hazel be able to explain all that Annie couldn't?

She leaned close to the porthole and took in the familiar skyline. A bittersweet smile twisted her lips when they passed the ferry dock. How long ago it seemed that she'd forced herself onto the ferry to begin her journey to Sutton Island.

The vessel eased into a berth. Annie stood and adjusted her hat, tugged her gloves on tighter, and picked up her valise. She could hardly believe how little she cared that she was on a boat. Evidently a broken heart was an excellent cure for an unreasonable fear. She supposed she had Noah Kennebrae to thank for helping her get over her terror of boats and water. . .and she had him to thank for the broken heart, too.

Stop it, Anastasia. Stop thinking about him and concentrate on what you're going to say to your father.

Even the gangplank gave her only a moment's unease. She nodded to the crewman and headed down the incline. Her boots hit the dock, her valise bumping against her leg.

A hand grabbed her elbow. "Anastasia." Her father's voice was like a breath of icy air in the late-June afternoon. "This way."

So, he'd come to meet her. She swallowed and dared a look at his face. His expression was as cold as his voice. His grip tightened, as if he feared she would disappear if he let go.

"Hello, Father." Guilt at the trouble and worry she'd caused him sat like a sodden stone in her chest. Her apology rushed out. "I'm sorry. I never should've—"

"For goodness' sake, Anastasia, not here. Wait until we get home." He took her valise and tugged her up the dock.

She trotted along behind, trying to hold her hat on. Shame heated her cheeks. No welcome, no thankfulness for her return. Instead she got a frigid reception and a reprimand for showing emotion in public.

They stopped beside a shiny new automobile. A chauffeur in a long white duster and driving gloves stood beside the curb. He stepped up to take the bag from her father's hand.

Her father held the back door and motioned to Anastasia. "Get in."

"Is this yours?" Anastasia gawked at the gleaming black paint and the shining windows. Her father had been skeptical of the newfangled automobiles and had resisted purchasing one before now.

"Of course. It arrived just after you left." He pursed his lips. "It won't bite you. Get in."

Anastasia gathered her skirts and ducked to enter the rear seat. Plush velvet yielded to her touch. She tried to make herself smaller when her father seated himself beside her. She couldn't help noticing the brass and wood, the wool carpet, even the crystal bud vases hanging on the divider between the front and back windows on each side. Work conveyance or not, her father had spared no expense when he finally decided to purchase an auto.

The chauffeur stepped to the front of the car and bent down to crank the engine to life. They jounced over the rough streets, heading up toward Michaelton House.

Anastasia gathered her courage for another try. She licked her dry lips. "Father, I apologize for running away. It was heedless of me. I should have stayed and spoken to you about your plans for me. I'm sorry I caused you such worry."

His fists tightened on his knees. Not once did he look her direction. "You *have* caused me worry, as well as a great deal of trouble. I should've known you'd do something harebrained like this. Do you have any idea how humiliating it was for me? Do you know the jeopardy you put my business reputation in? I did not enter into your marriage contract lightly, nor do I enjoy being made to look a fool. I'm lucky Abraham didn't cancel the contracts when he heard of your childish prank. It's a good thing your groom has been away recently."

"The wedding is still going to happen?" Anastasia's insides turned to water. "But I thought—"

"You *didn't* think, that's what. Yes, the wedding will happen, and you will be under lock and key until it does. When I think of all the trouble you've caused me, all the maneuvering I've had to do, I could shake you. I couldn't keep the story out of the papers. The police treated it like a kidnapping. Once I knew where you were and when you'd be returning home, I had to pay a steep 'fee' to an insufferable newspaper editor to have an article published saying you'd gone to visit friends. I looked like an imbecile, claiming not to know the traveling plans of my own daughter. But better that than the truth leaking out. From this moment on, you will not set foot outside Michaelton House unless you are in my presence. You will keep to your room and be thankful someone is still willing to marry you. If your fiancé saw you right now, he'd no doubt call off the wedding. I'm ashamed to admit you're my daughter, clothed like a servant, doing menial work. Your engagement party is tonight, and you will dress appropriately. After all, your betrothed will be present, and I'll be announcing your engagement."

Anastasia shrank back into her corner of the seat, her courage and will draining from her like beans from a sack. Nothing had changed in all the weeks she'd been away.

A fatalistic malaise came over her, pouring through the cracks of her broken heart. What did it matter now? The man she loved was marrying another. She might as well do the same.

੨ৱ

Her room was just as she had left it. White furniture with pale gold accents, light blue drapery on the canopy bed, gold rugs, white marble fireplace. The only thing missing was Hazel in the rocker. The emptiness enveloped Anastasia like a cold shawl.

She unpinned her hat, tugging it off and letting her hair straggle from its knot. The clock on the mantel ticked loudly announcing the time—just after five. Anastasia looked down at her humble dress. Brown wool skirt, sensible white blouse, unadorned brown jacket. So suitable for her life on Sutton Island, and so very wrong for a formal party in Duluth society. She decided against ringing for a maid to assist her.

During her preparations she prayed, tossed about in spirit between obedience to her father and brokenhearted loss and betrayal. She strove to cling to the serenity she had found at Sutton Island Light.

"Lord, thank You for being my strong tower. Help me to obey my father. Give me the strength to hold myself together when I meet this man I'm supposed to marry. Help me be gracious to him and obedient to my father."

The aromas of lilac sachets and cedar greeted her when she pulled open the wardrobe. Lavish gowns in silks and velvets hung on padded hangers, sleeves stuffed with tissue to hold their shape. What apparel would suit an engagement party? The fabrics, cool and soft, wrapped around her work-roughened fingertips. She'd need gloves tonight. Her gaze settled on a navy blue gown with golden stars sprinkled over the skirts and bodice. Perfect.

Two hours later, the butler knocked on her door. "Mr. Michaels requests your presence downstairs to receive your guests, miss."

Annie scanned her appearance once more, checking the heavily coiled braid and ostrich feathers at the back of her head, touching the pearl choker at her throat. With a final tug to her gloves, she opened the hallway door.

Male voices rose up the curved staircase, echoing against the ceiling and bouncing off the marble entryway.

She took extra care descending, stopping at the landing to bolster her courage before turning to go down the last, wide flight to the hall below. Somewhere down there, her husband-to-be waited. With a resigned and broken heart that longed to be back on Sutton Island, she walked down the stairs.

Halfway down, the voices stopped and the five men in the hall looked up.

Anastasia found herself staring into the blue eyes of Noah Kennebrae.

twenty

Anastasia froze on the stairway, her hand coming to her mouth too late to stop the cry of distress. It had never entered her head that her father might have the Kennebraes on the guest list. She tried to ignore how devastatingly handsome he looked in evening dress, how dear and familiar his features were to her. Did this mean he knew her fiancé? Worse yet, could he possibly be related to him?

He too seemed dumbstruck. His mouth opened, but no sound came out. Finally, he whispered, "Annie?"

The sound of her name on his lips shot through her like sparks. In spite of herself, she couldn't help but look for the woman who must be his betrothed. But the only other woman present was on the arm of a tall fellow who bore a slight resemblance to Ni—Noah Kennebrae.

Her father stalked to the bottom of the stairs and slammed his hands onto his waist. "Go back upstairs, Anastasia." His brows lowered, giving him a thundercloud look. "These people are leaving. According to the Kennebraes, the engagement is off. Noah Kennebrae asked for permission to tell you himself, but I won't allow him to humiliate you like this." He made shooing motions for her to go back up.

Her father's voice shook with anger when he turned toward the Kennebraes. "You'll rue the day you went back on your word, Kennebrae. I'll see the entire state knows you've broken our agreement."

Noah moved to the foot of the stairs until he stood directly in front of Anastasia. Tears pricked her eyes and heat skittered up her arms at having him so close. "*You're* Anastasia Michaels?"

She nodded, still unable to speak. She was so confused she couldn't catch and hold a single thought.

Noah turned to her father. "Sir, could you give us a few minutes alone to sort things out? Please?"

"Never. You've made yourself plain enough." Her father pounded up the steps and tugged on her arm, but she stood fast.

After a false start, she found her voice. "Nick. . .I mean, Noah. What are you doing here? What is my father talking about?" She moved down until she stood eye level with him, taking in every line of his face, searching for answers. "Tell me what's going on here."

He blinked and rubbed the palm of his hand across the nape of his neck. "If I knew, I'd tell you. It seems we've all gotten our lines crossed. Annie, I can't tell you how glad I am you're here. I was sick at heart when you weren't on the ferry this morning." He turned to Phillip Michaels. "Sir, we really need a few moments in private."

Father wasn't ready to be rational. "How dare you humiliate us this way! After all the work I went to getting Anastasia here in time for the party. I even borrowed your grandfather's yacht to go fetch her from that wretched island. Your grandfather promised the wedding would take place, no matter what, and you're in my house not five minutes before you want to call it all off? Get out of my house, the whole lot of you."

Before anyone could move, the butler opened the front door to a dozen or so party guests. Women in satin and jewels and men in evening dress, laughing, talking, and anticipating an enjoyable occasion, poured into the massive foyer.

Anastasia's father held fast to her elbow, his hand shaking. She dared a look up at him. His face set in hard lines, and his jaw muscles worked. They were trapped.

Anastasia's knees turned to pudding. She never should have come home. Once more she'd let her father down.

"Congratulations, Noah." A man with a florid complexion and the shoulders of a bear smacked Noah on the back. "'Bout time you put your neck into the matrimonial noose."

Noah took Anastasia's hand. He gave it a hard squeeze, as if to say, "*Play along and we'll sort it out later.*"

"Thank you, Titus. Allow me to introduce my bride-to-be, Anastasia Michaels. You know her father, Phillip." Noah flashed Anastasia a loaded look. "If you'll excuse us, we have a few matters to talk about privately."

"Oh no you don't, my boy. You'll have enough time to bill and coo later. Come meet some friends of mine." The man named Titus pulled Noah toward the door.

Noah glanced back over his shoulder as he was tugged away.

A beautiful brown-haired young woman introduced herself as Melissa Kennebrae, welcoming Annie to the Kennebrae family. Anastasia shook hands with Noah's brothers and briefly with Abraham Kennebrae himself. His dark eyes pierced her, taking her measure.

Father grabbed her elbow and leaned down to whisper harshly into her ear, "What is the meaning of this, Anastasia? Why did he call you Annie?" Father glowered at her, his eyes like hot coals. "Do you know each other?"

She swallowed, feeling as if she'd missed a step in the dark.

"I'm waiting for an explanation, Anastasia."

Rebellion flashed in her chest. "So am I. Why didn't you think to tell me the name of the man you were forcing me to marry? If I'd known. . ." Would it have changed anything? What game was Noah playing? Surely after all that had passed between them, he didn't think a wedding could take place? How could a marriage founded on lies and secrets and guilt ever work?

Anastasia found herself standing in a kind of receiving line, accepting congratulations and teasing remarks. Her father stood between her and Noah, his forbidding glare reminding her that a reckoning was coming. She'd never wanted to escape more. But where could she go?

"The name of the Lord is a strong tower: the righteous runneth into it, and is safe." Lord, help me. Be my strong tower in the middle of this storm.

More guests flocked in, and Anastasia got separated from her father and Noah. Everywhere she turned, another smiling face offered her best wishes.

How could this be straightened out? Duluth society filled the house, and not a soul knew of the lies, the sneaking around, the secret masquerade that stood like a wall between her and any future happiness. And Noah—when he thought this out, when he remembered how they'd deceived one another—she was sure he'd go through with calling things off.

As society matrons gathered around her, Anastasia watched Noah from the corner of her eye. He spoke to her father, whose eyes narrowed. But finally, when Father stalked down the hallway to his office, Noah followed close behind. No doubt Noah intended to explain all, after which someone would make an announcement that would end this farce.

She watched that door, ignoring everyone around her. After what seemed an age, Anastasia's father returned, looking like he'd bitten a wasp. Though she expected him to swoop down on her and hustle her upstairs with loud threats, he merely nodded to her.

Noah emerged, his face set in a determined expression. He marched straight up to Anastasia and took her hand. Ignoring comments and gasps from the onlookers, he pulled her down the hall to the room he'd just left. Anastasia had no choice but to trot in his wake.

Once inside the office, he released her hand and shut the door. He leaned against it and crossed his arms.

Anastasia didn't know what to think. So she just stood beside her father's desk and waited.

"You look beautiful. Blue suits you."

Her tongue sprang to life. "What a ridiculous thing to say at a time like this. What are we going to do? Half of Duluth seems to think we're getting married." Pain stabbed her heart.

He laughed. "Good. If I know my grandfather, by tomorrow, the other half will think so, too."

He'd obviously lost his wits. She twisted the diamond bracelet on her wrist, sliding it along her satin glove. "I've never seen my father so angry. He'll never forgive me."

"Don't worry about your father. I've had a word with him, and I think he understands. At least to the extent that he would rather have the marriage go ahead than everything to come out. He went to arrange for the toasts to be made. In fact, we only have a few minutes to get our lines uncrossed before someone breaks down this door and hauls us out to raise a glass of punch."

Tears pricked her eyes. "It's impossible. How could you even think of going forward with the engagement? You let me believe you were a fraud, that you had dallied with me then run off to marry another woman—" Her hands fisted at her sides.

When she tried to turn away from him, he pulled her into his arms. She pushed at him, struggling in his embrace, but he held on.

"Annie, stop it. Stop it!" He hugged her tight. "Let me explain."

"You can't. You can't explain anything. Do you know how much you hurt me?"

Sobs crowded her throat. As much as she wanted to loathe him, to lash out, to wound him, she couldn't.

When she stilled, he loosened his hold but didn't let her go. Instead he stroked her shoulders and hair, whispering against her temple. "I'm sorry, but hear me out." He put his finger under her chin and raised her face. "We have a lot of lines to untangle, but I want you to know I love you with all my heart, and I'd never knowingly hurt you. I had no idea who Grandfather was arranging for me to marry, and I certainly didn't think he'd go ahead with his plans after I left town."

She could barely take in his words. Too much heartbreak, too many guilty secrets stood between them. He said he loved her, but how could she be sure?

"Annie, please." He brushed a kiss across her forehead. "I don't want there to be any secrets between us ever again. I ran away from Duluth because I was ashamed. I felt so guilty over the wreck of the *Bethany*. I wanted to start a new life. But the guilt came with me. I thought I'd never be happy again. But then I met you. I've wanted to tell you the truth so many times. I wish now I had."

"You broke my heart when you left. You were engaged to someone else."

A smile tugged his lips. "Actually, when you think about it, I wasn't. I was engaged to you." He grasped her hands, his eyes pleading with her. "Annie, I promise you I was going to end the engagement my grandfather had arranged for me and find you as soon as possible. I don't want to spend another day without you. When you weren't on the ferry this morning, Eli had to nearly tie me down to keep me from setting sail for Sutton Island right then."

Hope leaped in her heart. "After everything, all the secrets, you still want to marry me? You're willing to forgive me for not telling you who I was and why I'd run away?"

"I'd be a real hypocrite if I didn't forgive you, wouldn't I? You had secrets from me. I had secrets from you. Annie, my love, I'm done with secrets. I'm done with being haunted by the past. From this moment on, I'm just Noah—Nick, if you prefer—forgiven by God, and I hope, by you. Say you forgive me for being so stupid as to walk away from you without telling you the truth. Say you love me as I love you.

And please, darling Annie, say you'll marry me." He stepped back and opened his arms, waiting for her response.

All the walls of hurt and hiding crumbled from around her heart. Without hesitation, she went into his embrace. "I do forgive you, and I do love you." Her heart pounded at admitting it aloud for the first time.

His eyes glowed with warmth and love, making her heart beat faster. "There's only one more thing I need to hear from you before I kiss you like I've been wanting to all night."

"And what's that?" She stroked her fingers down his cheek, delighting in the roughness of his stubbly whiskers. A stray thought flitted through her mind, wondering why he hadn't shaved. His question blew the thought from her mind.

"Anastasia Michaels, will you marry me?"

She cupped his cheeks and stared deeply into his blue eyes. "Noah Kennebrae, I would be honored." Her arms slipped around his neck.

He lowered his head and kissed her, lightly at first but then deeper. His kiss was everything she remembered and better.

When they pulled apart, he caressed her hair. "I love you, Annie. I don't think I can call you Anastasia. Will you mind? You'll always be Annie to me."

"I love you, too. I won't mind a bit, Nick." Her heart threatened to burst with happiness.

"Your father will be breaking down this door soon." He smiled into her eyes, pulling her close for another kiss, then rested his cheek on her hair. "There's only one thing that worries me."

"What?" She nestled her head under his chin, reveling in his embrace, almost weak from relief and joy.

"Do you have any idea how my grandfather is going to gloat? He's won again."

She smiled, hearing the laughter in his voice. "You don't sound like you mind very much."

A chuckle rumbled under her ear. "I don't suppose I do at

that. But when he hears the whole story of our little marriage masquerade, he's never going to let me live it down."

Annie sighed, loathe to return to the party. "Marriage masquerade. That's what it's been, hasn't it? But no more."

"No more, my love." He hugged her tight.

A Letter To Our Readers

Dear Reader:

In order that we might better contribute to your reading enjoyment, we would appreciate your taking a few minutes to respond to the following questions. We welcome your comments and read each form and letter we receive. When completed, please return to the following:

Fiction Editor
Heartsong Presents
PO Box 719
Uhrichsville, Ohio 44683

1. Did you enjoy reading *The Marriage Masquerade* by Erica Vetsch?
   - ❏ Very much! I would like to see more books by this author!
   - ❏ Moderately. I would have enjoyed it more if

   _____

   _____

   _____

2. Are you a member of **Heartsong Presents**? ❏ Yes ❏ No
   If no, where did you purchase this book? _____

   _____

3. How would you rate, on a scale from 1 (poor) to 5 (superior), the cover design? _____ _____

4. On a scale from 1 (poor) to 10 (superior), please rate the following elements.

_____	Heroine	_____	Plot
_____	Hero	_____	Inspirational theme
_____	Setting	_____	Secondary characters

5. These characters were special because? _____

_____

_____

6. How has this book inspired your life? _____

_____

_____

7. What settings would you like to see covered in future
   Heartsong Presents books? _____

_____

_____

8. What are some inspirational themes you would like to see
   treated in future books? _____

_____

_____

9. Would you be interested in reading other **Heartsong
   Presents** titles? ❏ Yes ❏ No

10. Please check your age range:
    ❏ Under 18   ❏ 18-24
    ❏ 25-34   ❏ 35-45
    ❏ 46-55   ❏ Over 55

Name _____

Occupation _____

Address _____

City, State, Zip _____

E-mail _____

THE HUSBAND TREE

Follow the trail to romance with ornery Belle Tanner and cantankerous cowboy Silas Harden, as they aim to avoid marriage while on a cattle drive.

Fiction, paperback, 320 pages, 5⅜" x 8"

Heartsong

Any 12
Heartsong
Presents titles
for only
$27.00*

HISTORICAL ROMANCE IS CHEAPER BY THE DOZEN!

Buy any assortment of twelve *Heartsong Presents* titles and save 25% off of the already discounted price of $2.97 each!

*plus $4.00 shipping and handling per order and sales tax where applicable.
If outside the U.S. please call
740-922-7280 for shipping charges.

HEARTSONG PRESENTS TITLES AVAILABLE NOW:

___HP652 *A Love So Tender*, T. V. Batman
___HP655 *The Way Home*, M. Chapman
___HP656 *Pirate's Prize*, L. N. Dooley
___HP659 *Bayou Beginnings*, K. M. Y'Barbo
___HP660 *Hearts Twice Met*, F. Chrisman
___HP663 *Journeys*, T. H. Murray
___HP664 *Chance Adventure*, K. E. Hake
___HP667 *Sagebrush Christmas*, B. L. Etchison
___HP668 *Duel Love*, B. Youree
___HP671 *Sooner or Later*, V. McDonough
___HP672 *Chance of a Lifetime*, K. E. Hake
___HP675 *Bayou Secrets*, K. M. Y'Barbo
___HP676 *Beside Still Waters*, T. V. Bateman
___HP679 *Rose Kelly*, J. Spaeth
___HP680 *Rebecca's Heart*, L. Harris
___HP683 *A Gentlemen's Kiss*, K. Comeaux
___HP684 *Copper Sunrise*, C. Cox
___HP687 *The Ruse*, T. H. Murray
___HP688 *A Handful of Flowers*, C. M. Hake
___HP691 *Bayou Dreams*, K. M. Y'Barbo
___HP692 *The Oregon Escort*, S. P. Davis
___HP695 *Into the Deep*, L. Bliss
___HP696 *Bridal Veil*, C. M. Hake
___HP699 *Bittersweet Remembrance*, G. Fields
___HP700 *Where the River Flows*, I. Brand
___HP703 *Moving the Mountain*, Y. Lehman
___HP704 *No Buttons or Beaux*, C. M. Hake
___HP707 *Mariah's Hope*, M. J. Conner
___HP708 *The Prisoner's Wife*, S. P. Davis
___HP711 *A Gentle Fragrance*, P. Griffin
___HP712 *Spoke of Love*, C. M. Hake
___HP715 *Vera's Turn for Love*, T. H. Murray
___HP716 *Spinning Out of Control*,
          V. McDonough
___HP719 *Weaving a Future*, S. P. Davis
___HP720 *Bridge Across the Sea*, P. Griffin

___HP723 *Adam's Bride*, L. Harris
___HP724 *A Daughter's Quest*, L. N. Dooley
___HP727 *Wyoming Hoofbeats*, S. P. Davis
___HP728 *A Place of Her Own*, L. A. Coleman
___HP731 *The Bounty Hunter and the Bride*,
          V. McDonough
___HP732 *Lonely in Longtree*, J. Stengl
___HP735 *Deborah*, M. Colvin
___HP736 *A Time to Plant*, K. E. Hake
___HP740 *The Castaway's Bride*, S. P. Davis
___HP741 *Golden Dawn*, C. M. Hake
___HP743 *Broken Bow*, I. Brand
___HP744 *Golden Days*, M. Connealy
___HP747 *A Wealth Beyond Riches*,
          V. McDonough
___HP748 *Golden Twilight*, K. Y'Barbo
___HP751 *The Music of Home*, T. H. Murray
___HP752 *Tara's Gold*, L. Harris
___HP755 *Journey to Love*, L. Bliss
___HP756 *The Lumberjack's Lady*, S. P. Davis
___HP759 *Stirring Up Romance*, J. L. Barton
___HP760 *Mountains Stand Strong*, I. Brand
___HP763 *A Time to Keep*, K. E. Hake
___HP764 *To Trust an Outlaw*, R. Gibson
___HP767 *A Bride Idea*, Y. Lehman
___HP768 *Sharon Takes a Hand*, R. Dow
___HP771 *Canteen Dreams*, C. Putman
___HP772 *Corduroy Road to Love*, L. A. Coleman
___HP775 *Treasure in the Hills*, P. W. Dooly
___HP776 *Betsy's Return*, W. E. Brunstetter
___HP779 *Joanna's Adventure*, M. J. Conner
___HP780 *The Dreams of Hannah Williams*,
          L. Ford
___HP783 *Seneca Shadows*, L. Bliss
___HP784 *Promises, Promises*, A. Miller
___HP787 *A Time to Laugh*, K. Hake

(If ordering from this page, please remember to include it with the order form.)

Presents